A Dead Lie

ALSO BY CLAIRE SHELDON

DETECTIVE JEN GARNER SERIES
Book 1: A Perfect Lie
Book 2: A Silent Child
Book 3: A Burning Lie
Book 4: A Dead Lie

A Dead Lie

CLAIRE SHELDON

Detective Jen Garner Book 4

Choc Lit

A JOFFE BOOKS COMPANY

Choc Lit

A Joffe Books company

www.choc-lit.com

First published in Great Britain in 2024

Cover art by Dee Dee Book Covers

ISBN: 978-1781898130

Lyn, Lu and Berni — three amazing ladies who made my dreams come true.

CHAPTER 1

Sean Sterling
Chessington Hospital, November 2021

'I got here as soon as I heard.'

The speaker, a youngish, well-dressed man, ran up to the reception desk in intensive care. 'Where is she? Is she okay?'

The nurse looked up at him, frowning. 'I'm sorry, sir, who were you wanting to see?'

'My wife!' he cried. 'She's been missing for forty-eight hours. The police have just rung me; they said she's had an accident and is in intensive care. I got here as soon as I could.'

'Can I take your name, please?'

'Sean Sterling. They said she was brought in a couple of days ago.'

Her eyes remained on the screen in front of her as she spoke. 'If you can just take a seat, Mr Sterling, I'll find someone to come and take you to your wife.'

He leaned over the desk. 'I need to see her.'

The nurse recoiled. 'Can I suggest you take a seat, sir? Otherwise, I'll call security and have you removed.'

As she spoke, the quiet was shattered by the blare of alarms. People appeared from nowhere and began to run through the doors leading into the ward.

'Mabel, he's crashing!'

At the sound of these words, the nurse leaped to her feet. She moved to follow the others into the ward, stopping only to address Sean once more before she left the room. 'Just wait there, sir. I'll find someone as soon as I can.'

This was stupid. He couldn't just stand here when his wife was inside. With a quick glance around the empty reception area, he stood on tiptoe and leaned over the counter. Still no one appeared, so he reached over and put his hand on the mouse. He was in luck — the nurse had been in such a hurry that she'd forgotten to lock the screen. He told himself he had a right to know how his wife was, if she was even here. He was her next of kin, after all.

CHAPTER 2

Jen Garner
2023

'Mum, tell him.' Melanie's screeching made Jen wince. Alex shouted something inaudible in reply. It was raining again. For two whole days, the kids had been shut up in school, unable to let off steam, and now things were heading for carnage.

Jen tried to concentrate on tidying the kitchen. James had rung her earlier saying he had to work late so could she pick up the kids. Meaning that she was left to deal with the chaos resulting from too many wet playtimes. She decided it was easier to just let the kids argue it out. Alternatively, she could chuck them both outside into the downpour.

She was loading the dishwasher when the doorbell rang. Who on earth was visiting at this time of the evening? Not James, surely; he had taken his keys with him. And it wasn't Max, her former boss and the kids' adoptive grandparent. He always called before popping over to see them.

With a sigh, Jen kicked the dishwasher closed and went to answer the door.

'Lisa, I need your help.' The woman's wet hair hung about her face. She wore no coat, just a T-shirt and jeans. Drops of rainwater splashed from her on to the doorstep.

Jen stared at her. There were very few people who knew her as Lisa. Unless this was . . .

'Chloe?'

'Please, Lisa. I had nowhere else to go.'

Nervous, Jen hesitated, but stepped aside. The woman entered. There was no way this was Chloe. Yet . . . she looked like Chloe. She sounded like Chloe. She even smelled like Chloe. But Chloe was dead.

CHAPTER 3

DI Chris Jackson

Since being ordered to take time off after the Carbon case three months ago, DI Chris Jackson hadn't been back to the station. He'd had messages from a couple of his colleagues checking that he was okay, and Greg had even appeared on his doorstep, which he didn't mind because Chris owed him an apology. He had told Greg that he'd been diagnosed with Multiple Sclerosis, and they'd chatted about life, Hannah, the team and the future.

It felt strange being back. He couldn't help feeling awkward about his new look, complete with the specs that he hoped made him look more intelligent. Whereas the walking stick just got in the bloody way. But this was his life now — oh, and the daily injections to keep the disease at bay, which only seemed to make him feel worse than ever. Gone was the Chris of former days, before Jen came along and everything changed.

'Morning, sir.' The officer greeted him as if he'd never been away.

'Morning, Officer Haskew.' Chris tapped his way through the double doors towards the lift that would take him up to his boss, Superintendent Gil Gray. He never used to take the lift.

Chris hadn't made his boss fully aware of what was going on with him. This was partly because Gil had made his feelings about the way the Carbon case had been handled known to all and sundry. As the lift door opened on the top floor, Chris took a deep breath. By now he was so used to pretending everything was okay that he'd forgotten how to be straight with anyone, let alone Gil Gray.

'Morning,' Chris almost sang. It sounded false, struck a wrong note.

'Ah, DI Jackson. Give me a minute, would you?' the Superintendent said. He was seated at his secretary's desk just outside his office.

'No Margaret today?' Chris asked.

'No, she retired, what, last week? Everything is in utter chaos. An agency temp was supposed to take over this morning, but she has failed to show. I hate to admit it, but I haven't a clue where anything is.' Both men chuckled. 'If you happen to know anyone who'd be interested in the job, I'm all ears.'

'My mum would love it, but I can't say I fancy working at the same place as my mother. Anyway, I'll have a think, sir.'

'Thanks, Chris. Now, come through to my office. I've ordered some tea and biscuits, and we can get down to business.'

'Thank you, sir.'

Leaning on his stick, Chris went in and, somewhat to his relief, made it to the chair in front of the Superintendent's desk without a single wobble.

'So, Inspector Jackson, I'm guessing you've come to discuss your return to work.'

'Yes, sir. I'm beginning to go stir-crazy stuck at home. Three months is a very long time to be staring at the same four walls.'

'But you've been resting, which is the most important thing you can do until you get this disease under control.'

'I don't think it'll ever be under control, sir.'

'Then maybe it's time for a career change,' Gil said.

'No!' Chris snapped, and immediately regretted it. 'Sorry, sir, it's just that policing is all I've ever wanted to do. I'm not about to let this stupid disease take it away from me.'

'I understand, Chris, I really do, but I can't have you on the streets if you're not fit for work.'

'I'm quite willing to take the fitness test, sir,' Chris said. 'I'm still fit for purpose.'

'Well, maybe we should look at a more office-based role for you?' Gil suggested.

'I had a feeling you were going to say that, sir. Much as I don't like the idea of being stuck in an office, you may be right. I can easily coordinate operations from my desk.'

'Then let's get occupational health in, and our HR department, and see how it can be arranged.'

'Sir.'

'Chris, on a personal note, if you ever need someone to talk to, my door is always open. I might be the big bad boss, but I hope you will also regard me as a friend.'

'Thank you, sir.' Chris was surprised at how well the meeting had gone. Slowly, he got to his feet, managing not to wobble. It was one of the things he was beginning to get used to.

'I'll get on to HR now and start the ball rolling,' Gil said.

'Thank you, sir,' Chris repeated. 'I'll just pop in and say hello to the team before I go.'

'As long as that's all you're doing, Inspector.'

CHAPTER 4

Jen Garner

The woman stood in the hallway, waiting, while all Jen could do was stare at her. 'Nice place,' she said eventually. Who was this person, and why the hell had Jen just invited her into the house, just because she looked like someone she used to work with?

'If you want to go through to the conservatory, I'll grab a towel so you can get yourself dry,' Jen said.

'Thanks, hun,' the woman replied.

Was it safe to leave this woman alone in her house? She had called her "Lisa", meaning that she must know who Jen had been in the past. Had she been sent to do her and her family harm? The kids were in their rooms; she could tell them to stay there as she went past. James was at work, in the pub or wherever, so he was safe. Quickly, she ran upstairs to the cupboard and grabbed a towel at random.

The woman looked relieved as Jen handed it over. 'I don't suppose you've got a spare set of clothes up there I can borrow?'

Jen decided it was time to take control of the situation. 'Who the hell are you?' she demanded.

'What do you mean?' The woman stared at her. 'Detective Chloe Seaward — your best friend, if I remember rightly.'

Jen rubbed unconsciously at the tattoo on her wrist. 'But you can't be.'

'Come on, Lisa. I don't get what you're playing at.' She nodded at Jen's wrist. 'Look.' The woman bent and rolled up the left leg of her jeans, revealing an identical tattoo on her ankle.

'But why come here? You've got a handler. Why didn't you contact them?' Jen said.

The woman shrugged. 'Your house was closer.'

'And how come you found out where I live?'

'Lisa, I don't understand why you're asking all these questions. I'm a detective. Of course I found out where you live.'

'Mum!' Jen jumped. In her confusion, she'd forgotten the kids.

'Hang on a minute,' Jen called. She turned to the stranger. 'I'll find you something to put on.'

Jen glanced at the clock. It was late, but this couldn't wait until the morning. There was one person who could tell her that this woman was definitely not Chloe.

CHAPTER 5

DI Chris Jackson

The office was deserted apart from Greg, who immediately pulled him into a bear hug. The warmth of it made Chris want to cry. Maybe this disease was making him an emotional as well as a physical wreck.

Greg stepped back and regarded him, smiling. 'I see you decided to stick with the glasses. I told you they made you look more intelligent.'

Chris grinned. 'It's my new persona.'

'Grab a chair and you can fill me in on how things are. We've all been so worried about you,' Greg said.

'Nothing to tell since I saw you. I'm in the process of getting myself signed back on duty.'

Greg laughed. 'And how's that going?'

Chris avoided the question. 'Where is everyone anyway?'

'Jen left early; she had to pick up the kids. Julie and Colin are out somewhere on a case, and as for Trudie—' Greg shrugged — 'your guess is as good as mine.'

'Everything as usual then.'

'Always. I'm sorry to cut this short, boss.' Greg pulled his phone out of his pocket and stared at the screen. 'The wife booked me a dentist appointment that I've been trying to avoid for the past six months, so I'd better go before they strike me off.'

'Not a problem. I was only visiting. It's not like I don't know my way around.'

Greg beamed at him as he put his coat on. 'We'll have to catch up soon, boss.'

'I'm sure we'll have plenty of time for that once I'm back.'

Chris watched Greg hurry off, leaving him standing in an empty room. He looked around. This place had been the hub for every major crime he had been involved in since he joined the team. Well, they seemed to be running things pretty smoothly without him. Shaking off a pang, he decided he might as well pop into his office and then get back home to the cat and the box set of *Breaking Bad* that Hannah had told him he just had to watch.

His office was just as he had left it. No magic fairy had come in and cleaned, and they had definitely not done his outstanding paperwork. After a quick look round, Chris placed the framed photo of his adopted donkey on his desk. Others might have displayed a photo of their loved one, or their kids, but not him. Oh no, he had a photo of a donkey . . .

11

CHAPTER 6

Adam Coulthard
October 2021

I never realised how much I loved Chloe until she was gone, taken from me in the course of her undercover work for them. Jen had promised to keep in touch, saying we could meet up now and then to reminisce about the woman we'd both loved. But once the case had been closed and the funeral held, she stopped calling. She went back to her nice, cosy second life and I was left to grieve alone. I spent my days in front of the television smoking dope. I didn't need to deal drugs anymore as I had Chloe's life insurance payment and a fat pension, but the more my boredom intensified the more I smoked. That was my life.

Out of the blue I received an invitation to meet one of my old associates down in London. He'd just come out of jail after serving a sentence for dealing to minors. I was no longer interested in dealing, but I decided what the hell, I had nothing better to do, so I might as well go. I arranged to meet up with him in a place called Chessington, and that's where I first caught sight of her.

I never got to see Chloe's body. I was enough of a dupe to believe them when they'd told me she was dead. But seeing her reminded me of who she'd worked for and I began to wonder if they'd faked her death. Maybe it was part of some undercover operation that even the great Jen Garner didn't know about.

Her hair was longer and hung lank about her face. She'd put on a great deal of weight too, but it was Chloe all right. My Chloe, strolling across Chessington marketplace as if she didn't have a care in the world. I never got to meet my friend for his first drink out on licence. Instead, I followed Chloe. I had to tell her that I'd never given up hope, that I still loved her, and how much I missed her. I wanted her to know that I'd sent that necklace to Jen just as she asked me to. That I wanted her to come back home where she belonged. We'd have the wedding of our dreams, and the two kids we'd stayed up all night planning for.

CHAPTER 7

Sean Sterling
November 2021

'Can I help you?' A different nurse arrived at the reception desk and started moving stuff around.

Sean leaped up from his seat. 'Hi, yes. My wife was brought in a couple of days ago,' he said. His surreptitious look at the computer had confirmed that she was definitely here, and now he needed someone to take him to her.

'Ah, Jane Doe . . .'

'Yes, the police phoned me earlier to tell me they'd found her.'

'We'd been wondering when someone would come asking after her.' The nurse's attention was still on the desk.

'She went missing, you see. Two days ago. I've been out of my mind with worry.'

'Well, at least you know she's safe, Mr, er . . .'

'Sterling. Sean Sterling.'

'Right, Mr Sterling, if you'd like to follow me. Oh, and can you give me the name of the officer who contacted you so we can let them know you've arrived?'

'Yes, of course. It was an Officer Pinkington. He phoned me earlier. He said my wife had been involved in an accident.'

'Yes, I'm afraid she isn't in a good way.' The nurse led the way past rooms where people lay hooked up to ventilators, many surrounded by family or hospital staff.

'I guessed as much when I was told she was in intensive care.' He shook his head. 'And she's been lying here all this time without me knowing. I'm guessing she isn't conscious?'

The nurse held open yet another door. 'I'm afraid she is in a coma.'

'How long has she been like that?' he asked.

'Look, I'm not the best person for you to be asking. As soon as I've got you to your wife, I'll find a doctor who can explain her situation.'

'Thank you.' He followed her along in silence, looking into every bay he passed.

"Okay, Mr Sterling, she's just in there. Now, before you go in, please use the hand sanitiser and put on one of these aprons, shoe protectors and a mask. We don't want to expose your wife to any infection, do we?'

'Of course. Thank you so much for taking me to her. I hope the person Mabel rushed off to assist is okay?'

The nurse's smile revealed nothing as he struggled with the shoe protectors. 'I'm afraid I can't comment on that.'

'God, these aren't easy to put on, are they?'

'Okay, Mr Sterling, you're free to go in when you're ready.'

Sean pushed open the door, walked into the room and gasped. 'Oh my God, Chloe. What the hell happened to you?' Like many of the other patients, his wife was fitted with a ventilator, she had a bandage around her head and her eyes were swollen and bruised. 'I'm so, so sorry, Chloe. I wish I could have found you sooner. I promise I will never leave you again.'

CHAPTER 8

Max Collins
2023

'I got here as soon as I could,' Max said.

'I'm so confused, Max,' Jen said. 'I don't know what to think.'

'It's okay, Jen, I'll sort this.' Max strode into the hallway. 'So, where is she?'

'She's in the conservatory. I've been trying to keep her away from the kids, just in case.'

'You'd better go and make sure they're okay,' Max said.

'They'll be down as soon as they hear your voice.' Jen made for the stairs to head them off.

The woman stood up as he walked in. 'Look, Max, I know I broke the rules. I should've contacted my handler, but Lisa's was closer and I needed to get dry and warm.'

'Who the hell are you?' Max asked.

'What do you mean, who am I? I'm Chloe Seaward, of course.'

'See, I'm having difficulty believing that because Chloe died two years ago.'

'What can I do to make you believe that I am who I am? There's our matching tattoos. I've shown Lisa mine. You've got to believe me.'

'Chloe Seaward was beaten and left for dead. She was identified by her DNA. DNA doesn't lie, so who are you?' Even as he spoke, he was beginning to wonder. Jen was right — this woman looked and sounded exactly like Chloe. 'If you're who you say you are, you've completely broken protocol. You know what to do if you're in trouble.'

'But . . . but here was closer, and I knew Lisa would be able to help me without throwing everyone into a panic.'

'J— I mean Lisa hasn't been in the service for, what, thirteen years? How do you know you weren't followed? How do you know you haven't led someone here? The Chloe Seaward I knew wouldn't put anyone at risk, let alone her best friend. So, I'm going to ask you one more time, who are you?' Max's face had turned red. He could hear his doctor telling him to take things more easily before he had a heart attack.

'I'm Detective Chloe Seaward. I've been undercover for over three years, following the Crawford drugs syndicate. I directed Dana Anwar to you, or have you forgotten the child abuse ring she helped close down?'

Max was beginning to feel as confused as Jen. 'I'm having some difficulty believing you when I've seen the DNA evidence. Chloe is dead.'

The woman sat down. She looked exhausted, deflated. 'I don't know what else I can say to make you believe that I am who I say I am.'

'You've got to understand the position you've put us all in,' Max said.

'I do, boss, but I was out of options.'

'Do I need to move Lisa and her family to a secure location? Is she now in danger, her whereabouts known?' Max demanded.

'No, sir. I made sure I wasn't followed. Lisa and her family are safe.'

Suddenly the front door banged. 'Jen, you will not believe the day I've had,' James called out.

'Stay there,' Max warned, but Jen got there first.

'James, you're home.'

CHAPTER 9

DI Chris Jackson

'Honey, I'm home,' Chris announced. It was his little private joke with himself. No one other than the cat was waiting for him. Thankfully, the cleaners would be long gone by now; he wasn't in the mood for company. All he wanted was to sit and watch *Breaking Bad* and forget his problems. Though they had a habit of reminding him.

As he took off his shoes and propped his stick against the wall, he noticed a pair of Hannah's heels. Hmm. Maybe the cleaners had found them lying around. As he opened the door to the living room, he heard the rapid tap of fingers on a keyboard.

'I thought I heard you come in,' Hannah said.

'What the hell are you doing here?'

'I told you, didn't I? I said I'd be here when you got back from seeing your boss.'

'Yeah, and I told you that you didn't need to be. It was just an informal chat.'

Hannah stood up and kissed him. 'Oh, you'll never guess who I met today.' She began jiggling on the spot like a small eager child.

'Now let me see . . . The King?'

'Oh no, more important than that. Your cleaners,' she said. Chris rolled his eyes. 'Oh God.'

'I don't think they knew who I was when I let myself in, but once I explained that I was your girlfriend, they were like, "Ah".'

'So I can say goodbye to my pretence of leading a bachelor lifestyle.'

She grinned. 'Like you were ever any good at it.'

'You wait. When it's time to pay their wages, they'll be asking if I still need their services.' Hannah threw a cushion at him.

Chris couldn't decide whether he was happy to find her here, or whether he'd rather sit and brood.

'Coffee?' Hannah called from the kitchen.

'Decaf, please.'

'That stuff tastes disgusting,' she said.

'You were there when my consultant told me I should think about cutting down on the caffeine.'

'And you were there when I asked him if he'd ever tried decaf coffee.' Chris suspected his consultant probably drank more of the stuff than he did. At least he hoped he did.

Chris watched as Hannah busied herself in the kitchen. He also noticed that his cat was asleep on a chair in the living room. Fluff and Hannah must have come to an agreement then. Chris wondered if it had something to do with the bag of Dreamz treats and the catnip he'd seen poking out of Hannah's bag once. Which was okay with him; at least the two females in his life were getting on.

He took a seat at the kitchen table. 'You got much on?' he asked.

'As always. I'm hoping Sam will have finally decided what she wants to do, because I can't keep her on the team if she's too scared to go out into the field.'

'I'm sorry.' In a way, it was Chris's fault that Sam was reacting so badly. If he had handled the situation better, Sam would never have been put in the position of having to fire a gun and injure someone.

Hannah shrugged. 'Yeah, well, she needs to either get out there or quit.'

'Is there anything I can do to, you know, help her out a bit? Seeing as it's kind of my fault.'

'I don't know, Chris, I really don't. Find her a new job? Don't get me wrong, the service is happy to keep paying her private medical bills. It's just—'

'You need someone who's able to go out in the field at a moment's notice and not panic,' he said.

'Correct. Look, as much as I hate to break up our happy reunion, I'm afraid I've got work to do.' Hannah passed him a mug.

'For you, dear, anything.'

* * *

He'd no idea he'd been asleep until the warm spot from the cat disappeared to be replaced by a heavier one, and he was enveloped in her perfume. His body began to do that thing it always did when she was that close.

'Wakey wakey, Detective Inspector,' she whispered seductively in his ear, followed by 'Argh,' as the sound of "The Imperial March" filled the room.

Hannah fumbled for her phone. 'Max? What? No, I'm in Derby, at Chris's.'

Chris sat up. Something had happened.

'Yeah, I can get over to Jen's. Why? Is everything okay?' A pause, the tinny sound of Max's voice. 'Give me half an hour and I'll be over.'

'What's up?' Chris asked.

'I need to get over to Jen's. Chloe Seaward has just turned up.'

He stared at her. 'But she's dead.'

CHAPTER 10

Chloe Seaward

'Look, can I at least get a shower or something?' Chloe said. 'I'm cold, and I've been in these wet clothes all day.'

Max and Lisa were still standing at the door, whispering. Lisa glanced at him and shrugged. 'I suppose she can use the bathroom downstairs.'

Why did they keep referring to her as "she"? 'It'll be just like old times,' she tried, but received no response. 'Max, I really don't understand what the problem is.'

'As I've told you, the problem is that Chloe Seaward is dead.' Max sighed as he rubbed his hands together. 'You know the way we work. Not only have you broken protocol, but you've turned up on Lisa's doorstep, putting her and her family at risk. I shouldn't have to repeat those.'

'But—'

Max held up his hand. 'No buts. Until we figure this out, you're someone unknown to us, and we'll treat you as such.'

She sighed. None of this made sense. Instead of the expected welcome, her best friend and her boss were both treating her like some kind of criminal. She was tired, tired of running. Tired of the endless struggle.

'The bathroom is through there.' Lisa pointed to the kitchen.

'Thanks, hun. I . . . I'm sorry it's come to this.'

But all Lisa said was, 'Shout if you need anything.'

Inside the bathroom she saw the kids' shampoo on the window ledge. She opened the top and inhaled the fresh scent of apple, transporting her back to her childhood, and memories of home.

CHAPTER 11

Hannah Littlefair

Hannah marched through the door, straight into the kitchen, where Max stood waiting.

'How come you're up here and not down in London?' Jen asked.

'It was supposed to be a booty call, but it looks like you've put a dampener on that.' Hannah laughed as she embraced Jen.

Max smirked. 'Keeping a check on our DI's health?'

'How is Chris?' Jen asked.

'Getting there,' Hannah replied. 'You know Chris. Anyway, what's this about Chloe Seaward turning up on your doorstep?'

'All I did was finish work early so I could pick the kids up from school, and now I find myself with some woman in my downstairs bathroom claiming that she's Chloe. I've sent James upstairs. He's watching TV with the kids.'

'And we've got one great big security breach,' Max said.

'So, what's the plan?' Hannah was so used to taking orders from Max that she automatically turned to him.

'You tell me. You're the boss. I was hoping to get back for my book club, but I don't see that happening now.' Max pulled out his phone.

Hannah pinched the bridge of her nose in exasperation. 'Let me get this straight. This person is claiming to be Chloe, who we know for a fact to be dead.'

'Yep. We have her DNA. A sample was taken when her body was brought back to us,' Max said.

'Okay, and what has she said? What do you think?' Hannah looked from one of them to the other.

'Well, this is the thing,' Jen said. 'She mentioned the trafficking case and the child abuse ring. She keeps calling me Lisa, but she never knew me as Jen. And she didn't seem to think it at all strange that she should have tracked me down, since, in her words, she's a detective.'

'So she even thinks she's Chloe?' Hannah asked.

'Yes, but she can't be, can she? Chloe's dead,' Max said.

Just then, James came into the kitchen. 'I'm sorry to break up the party, but I really need a drink. Everything okay, is it?'

'Hi, James,' Hannah said. 'We're just trying to work out who our mystery guest is.'

'Who does she say she is?' James asked.

'Chloe Seaward,' Hannah said.

James gasped. 'What? *The* Chloe Seaward?'

'That's why I need you to keep an eye on the kids. Keep them out of the way until we can get her out of here,' Jen said.

He smiled. 'Chocolate and *Toy Story 3* for the ninety millionth time it is then.'

'Thank you.' Jen kissed his cheek.

They all stood and stared at the woman who emerged from the bathroom. Her hair was messy and wet, and Jen's clothes were far too big for her, but she looked exactly like Chloe.

'Oh, look, more people come to stare at me,' she said. 'My, James, haven't you aged well.'

James appeared to be lost for words. But it was written all over his face: this was Chloe Seaward.

25

'Hannah Littlefair. We worked together briefly at one point.' Hannah stepped forward, breaking the spell that seemed to have fallen on them all.

'Ah, I thought it was you. What are you doing up here?' the woman said.

'Trying to figure out who the hell you really are,' Hannah replied.

The woman sighed. 'You'll be bringing out Adam next.'

'A lot has happened since *Chloe* was last in the office,' Hannah said. 'Max has retired and moved up here, and I'm now in charge.'

'How did you manage that?' the woman asked with a smile.

Hannah grinned despite herself. 'Ways and means.'

'Is Sam still PA?' the woman asked.

'Enough!' Jen cried. 'You all seem to be forgetting that I have two small people upstairs who it's my duty to protect. So let's cut the bullshit, shall we? Who are you really? And what dangers have you brought to my door?'

CHAPTER 12

Chloe Seaward

'I'm so sorry about this,' James said from the door to the conservatory.

'It's okay, I understand.' In truth, she didn't understand a thing. In the kitchen they were arguing about what to do with her. Maybe she shouldn't have come. Maybe she should have just sucked it up and got in touch with her handler. Who, she was forced to admit, she hadn't contacted in far too long. No doubt she'd be in trouble for that too. Maybe that was why they thought she was dead.

'If you ask me, this is totally embarrassing, whoever you are,' James said. 'I'd offer to get you a drink or something, but I daren't go into the trenches. I'd probably be shot.'

'It's all good. I've had a shower and the chance to get dry. By the way, how did your mate's wedding go?' James looked puzzled. 'I first met you thirteen years ago, if you remember. You were at your mate's stag do.'

Light dawned. 'Oh yeah. Of course. The night I met Jen. The wedding was great, thanks. A lot of heavy drinking went on after, if I remember rightly.'

'Jen? Oh, is that what she was calling herself back then?' she said.

For a brief moment, James seemingly met her confusion with his own, but almost immediately his expression resolved into a blank stare. 'Something like that.'

'So, how does it feel to be part of the Met family?' she asked.

'The Met family?'

'Doesn't Lisa work with Max and Hannah? I thought she'd come back and take Max's job when he retired.'

'I think I've said too much,' James muttered.

Hannah marched into the room. 'Chloe — or whoever you are — as I'm sure you appreciate, your arrival has caused a bit of confusion, and given how late it is, there isn't much we can do about it now.'

'Okay.' Chloe waited.

'Assuming you've got nowhere to go, I'm going to arrange a room in a hotel for the night. Tomorrow, we can work out what we do next.'

'Sounds good to me. I'm clearly not welcome here.' She glanced at James, who was suddenly very busy on his phone.

'Thank you for your understanding,' Hannah said. 'I'll see if I can get you into the one I'm staying at.'

A grim realisation struck her. 'So you can keep an eye on me.'

Hannah turned and walked out of the conservatory, past James, who was still standing in the doorway. She suddenly realised that he'd been posted on guard duty. For God's sake, what did they think she was going to do?

CHAPTER 13

Sean Sterling
November 2021

A rather smart-looking man came into the room, followed by a second man in a white coat. He introduced himself as Dr Rohampton, his colleague as Dr Smalley.

Sean scrambled to his feet and said hi.

'I'm so glad the police have found someone from this poor lady's family,' Dr Rohampton said.

Sean took the offered hand. 'Not half as relieved as I was when I got the call. I've been going out of my mind with worry.'

'Well, you're here now. That's all that matters. May I ask what the lady's name is?'

'Chloe. We've only recently been married, so when she disappeared, I thought she might have changed her mind and left me or something.'

'I expect the police will have a few questions for you.'

'Where was she found? What happened to her?' Sean asked.

'Chloe suffered a serious head injury. We needed to operate immediately to reduce the swelling. She's been in a coma following her surgery.'

29

Sean winced. 'Was she conscious when they brought her in?'

'Yes, but her speech was slurred, which was why we had to operate as soon as we could.'

'What caused her injury?'

The doctor consulted his notes. 'She was brought into A & E following a road traffic accident.'

'Oh, poor, poor Chloe.' Sean's voice shook with emotion. 'Will she . . . will she come back to me?'

Dr Smalley stepped forward. 'We've done all we can. It's just a matter of time now, while we wait for her brain to heal and for her to regain consciousness.'

Sean sat down suddenly, as if it were all too much. 'Any idea how long that will take?'

'Unfortunately we are unable to give a timeframe for cases like these. As you can see, she is being closely monitored.'

'Will she have brain damage?' Sean asked.

'Again, we won't know until she regains consciousness. All I can say for now is that the indications are fairly positive.'

'Oh, Chloe . . .'

'We just need to examine her, and then I'll get a nurse to come in and answer any questions you may have.' While Sean watched, they opened her eyes and shone a light into them, took a reading of her heart rate and lifted the bandage up to check how her head wound was healing. 'We'll need to get a fresh dressing on this wound,' Dr Smalley said to his colleague.

'Yes, it's been a while since it was last cleaned.' They proceeded to murmur in hushed tones, using terms Sean failed to understand.

'What's her prognosis, doc?'

'Her obs are pretty stable,' Dr Smalley replied.

That doesn't answer my question, Sean thought, though he was wary of making himself too much of a nuisance.

'Mr Sterling, we're having problems locating your wife's medical records. Would you be able to help us? Who is her GP?' Dr Rohampton asked.

'Oh, I thought they were all computerised now.'

'Unfortunately, there is still a massive backlog from before 2008,' the doctor said.

'That'll explain it then. My wife was very fit and never went to a doctor.'

Dr Rohampton frowned. 'Do you happen to know her NHS number by any chance?'

'No, sorry, but I can look for it when I get home.'

'If you could, Mr Sterling. It would help us treat her.'

'I will, thank you. Thank you so much.'

'Could you also give us your wife's maiden name and any previous address. Maybe we could search that way?' Dr Smalley suggested.

'Seaward. We never changed our surnames when we married. My wife is very independent and didn't believe that a wife should necessarily take her husband's name. And neither of us fancied a double-barrelled one. Plus, Chloe often said that marriage was just a piece of paper that didn't mean anything. I can find our marriage certificate if that would help?'

'Okay, that would be helpful. In the meantime, we'll keep on searching for her records. Thank you, Mr Sterling.' Dr Smalley made a note on the clipboard hanging at the foot of her bed.

'Keep talking to her, Mr Sterling. The latest research says that patients in a coma may be able to hear what is being said to them,' Dr Rohampton said.

'Can I hold her hand?' Sean asked.

'Of course. Just be careful of the tubes, won't you?'

'Thank you so much for looking after her. I don't know what I'd do without her.'

CHAPTER 14

DI Chris Jackson
2023

'Hey, I was wondering when I'd hear from you.'

Finally, Chris had a call from Hannah. She had been gone for hours and he wasn't sure if she'd be back anytime soon. That was the thing with Hannah. Sometimes she would disappear for days on end and then turn up as soon as he'd stopped waiting. It was part of her job and he accepted it. In the beginning, he'd found it rather exciting, but the more serious their relationship grew, the more he worried. Where was she, what was she doing and, most importantly, was she safe?

'Things have got rather complicated. Fancy a night in one of Long Eaton's premier hotels?' she said.

He chuckled. 'Sounds romantic.'

'I need your help with something.'

'You're not trying to drag me into another case? You know what happened last time I worked a case with you.'

'We both also know how much you enjoyed it.' Hannah's voice was low. Chris could picture her giving him "that" look.

'What's cracking off anyway?' Chris grimaced at his unsuccessful attempt to sound businesslike.

'Meet me at the Conway in Long Eaton in an hour and I'll tell you all about it.'

* * *

He stood outside the Conway, waiting to meet Hannah. How the hell could Chloe Seaward possibly be alive? He had been there when her body was found. He clearly remembered the way she'd been lying and had seen what they'd done to her before dumping her body into the water. It was in the same position as Daisy, the victim of one of his unsolved cases, had been left all those years go. So how could she have turned up on Jen's doorstep?

'Inspector Jackson?'

He jumped. 'Sam, what are you doing here?'

'When the mistress calls, the minions come running.' Sam laughed.

'Where *is* the mistress?'

'She asked me to meet you and give you the card to your room — oh, and your briefing documents.' Sam handed him a sealed envelope.

'Let me guess. I need to eat it as soon as I've read it.'

'Or maybe it'll self-destruct.'

'It wouldn't surprise me.' Chris took a laptop from his bag and handed it to Sam. 'You'd better give her this. If she asks about the cat's footprints, just deny they are there.'

'Ah, the cat. Her nemesis . . .'

'I've no idea what you're talking about,' he said. 'Are you staying here tonight?'

'In Long Eaton's newest hotel? I should be so lucky.'

He grinned. 'Van in the car park?'

Sam's face again cracked with mirth. 'Bit more upmarket. Jen's sofa.'

'It'll probably be more homely than here,' Chris said.

'Well, I'll see you in the morning, Inspector. Don't get up to anything I wouldn't.'

'Me? No chance.'

Chris made his way into the hotel. The Conway, converted from one of the many empty buildings in Long Eaton, had only recently been opened. It certainly oozed class, but would it draw that sort of clientele to the town? With three hotels already situated close to the junction with the M1, he doubted it would tempt people to venture any further. He opted, for the exercise, to take the stairs to the second floor, found his room and made straight for the mini-bar. Sod it. If the service were paying for the room, he'd make the most of it.

He kicked off his shoes and sat on the bed, where he opened the envelope Sam had given him:

> *Chris, I need you to follow this lady while she is staying at the hotel tonight. She is claiming to be Chloe Seaward but as of yet we haven't been able to prove whether or not it's her. Some of the things she has said have surprised us. Observe her while she's in and around the hotel, but under no circumstances must you approach her.*
>
> *Once she is in her room and the coast is clear, you'll find me in room 304.*
>
> *Hannah*

Chris pulled out the picture that Hannah had included with the brief. *Holy shit.* Chloe Seaward was looking back at him. If he hadn't seen her dead body, he'd have been certain it was her. He knew just what Hannah had done — as soon as he'd seen the picture, he'd want to check this Chloe out for himself. She had him hook, line and sinker. As for a night in room 304, it was late, and he was tired.

CHAPTER 15

Jen Garner

Jen was sitting at the table, her head on her arms.

'I just don't understand.'

'What I found really weird was her asking me about Jake's wedding,' James said. Max, Hannah and the woman had left, in their place an unmarked police car outside the house "just in case".

'I was told she was dead. I knew she was. I found her killer, for God's sake. How could she have turned up on the doorstep?' Jen got up abruptly, opened the fridge and pulled out a second bottle of wine. 'It just doesn't make sense.'

'Jen, that's not going to solve anything.' James stood up and gently took the bottle from her.

'She kept saying all these things that only Chloe would know, like Dana and the Teddington case. No one but her knew about those.'

'And she kept referring to you as Lisa,' James added. 'Didn't Chloe know you were now called Jen?'

'I don't remember, James. And what's more, if she *is* Chloe, then who was the dead woman?'

35

James reached out and wiped her tears with his thumb. 'What did Max say? I heard you guys arguing.'

'He said what he always says. It will all be sorted tomorrow.' She grunted.

James pulled her into a hug. 'He's never let you down though, has he?'

'There's always a first time.' She gripped him tightly. 'Oh, to stay here for ever.'

'Always, Mrs Garner, always.'

'Shall I just stay here? I really don't want to go swanning off to London with the others. Maybe I should refuse? What do you think?'

'I can't answer that one for you, Jen. You must do whatever's right for you,' he said.

'I know.' She sighed. 'Let's pack the bags and do a moonlight flit. Go somewhere warm.'

'And what about work? And the kids have school,' he said.

'Yeah, work. That's gonna be a problem wherever I run off to.'

'Work?' James echoed.

'The Superintendent has given me any number of warnings. Chris is still off sick so we're already a man down and I'm going to want leave with immediate effect.'

'The team will understand, won't they?'

'I don't know, James. They're all overworked too, what with Chris not being there.' Jen pulled away from him, looking around as her phone began to ring.

'Let it go to voicemail. It's late; it can wait till tomorrow,' James said.

'I can't, James. It might be important.'

'There's your answer then.' He turned away from her.

Jen found her phone in the living room. 'It's Hannah. She's wondering if Sam could stay over tonight.'

James raised his eyes to the ceiling. 'Why do we have to go through this every time? Just when I think that for once you've changed your mind and are staying at home, something happens and you're off again.'

CHAPTER 16

Jen Garner

'Here.' Jen handed Sam a cup of hot chocolate topped with cream and marshmallows.

'Thank you so much for letting me stay, Jen.'

'It's not a problem, Sam. I'm just sorry I can't put you anywhere better than the sofa.'

'It's fine, hun.' Sam sipped at the drink. She looked pale and tired, nothing like the young woman Jen had met when she first returned to the service. Looking at her now, you would never believe her capable of firing a gun at a suspect, yet just over a year ago that's exactly what she had done.

'I'll try and make sure the kids don't race in and disturb you in the morning.'

'I can't wait to meet them.' The thought of meeting Jen's kids brought a look of animation to Sam's drawn features.

'Sam, what's going on with you?' Jen asked.

She shrugged. 'I'm good.'

'You sure? How are you finding being on the other side of the desk?'

'Hannah still asks me to type stuff.' Sam carefully picked out a marshmallow. 'It was good seeing Chris. I'd been so worried about what to say to him, and—'

'I bet he was glad to see you, too.'

'When Hannah told me about his diagnosis, I was like, is this the end for him? You know, his career. Him and Hannah. I mean, she can be a real whirlwind, and to be in a relationship with someone . . .'

'When you have a life-altering disability,' Jen finished.

'Right.'

'Well, I've not seen much of him since his diagnosis, but Hannah seems to think he is doing okay.'

'I keep thinking, what if I'd shot him? I would never have been able to forgive myself.'

Jen laughed. 'I don't think he'd have been too impressed either. But you didn't. You hit the wall, which was the right thing to do.'

'Um, how did you cope, Jen? I mean, when you were out in the field.'

'What do you mean "cope"?'

'While I was Max's PA, I used to see you all rushing in and out, and every one of you looked like you were having the time of your life.' She paused. 'And then I finally get my chance to go out too, and what happens? I almost shoot a fellow officer. I just can't get it out of my mind. You must have had things like that happen to you too, but you're fine.'

'I'm not sure I'm all that fine.' Jen chuckled. 'The times when you saw us rushing in and out, we were usually on an adrenaline-fuelled high. We weren't like that all the time, you know. We had some really bad moments out there.'

'So I was seeing what you did in the field through rose-tinted glasses, is what you're saying,' Sam said.

'I know I might come across as a super detective, but I nearly lost my family not so long ago. Running into a burning building didn't go down too well either.'

For the first time, Sam smiled. 'I knew it was you when I heard it on the news.'

'You enjoyed being Max's PA, didn't you?' Jen said.

'Yeah, I loved it.'

'Come into work with me tomorrow.'

'Okay.' Sam looked surprised.

'I've got to go in and ask for time off, and there is someone I'd like you to meet.'

'I'm sorry, I've kept you up late,' Sam said.

'Don't worry about it.' Jen turned to leave the room.

'Jen?'

'Hmm?'

'Do you think it's really her? Could it be Chloe?'

CHAPTER 17

DI Chris Jackson

He'd never enjoyed those zombie movies, and certainly didn't believe in the walking dead. Chris was a police officer; he put his faith in hard facts and what the pathologists told him. Yet here, sauntering through the hotel bar towards him, was the living embodiment of Chloe Seaward.

He blinked. All he needed to do was watch, and she certainly wasn't easy to miss. The eyes of most of the men in the hotel bar followed her progress across the room. Tomorrow, no doubt, she would be subjected to a barrage of tests to prove her true identity. But if she did turn out to be Chloe, who the hell was the dead woman?

'Mind if I join you?'

He jumped as she went to take the empty seat next to him. 'Oh, sure.' He could already imagine the look on Hannah's face when he told her the mystery woman had been chatting up her spy.

'I'm Chloe, by the way,' she said.

'Chris. So, what brings you to Long Eaton?'

'Just visiting a friend. You?'

'I'm supposed to be meeting someone too, but it looks like I've been stood up.'

She laughed. 'Oh dear. Sure you don't mind me joining you?'

'No, it's fine.'

'I just find that people always assume that a woman sitting alone in a bar is either a hooker or needs chatting up.'

Chris immediately wondered if he was ever guilty of this very thing. 'Well, you're welcome to sit with me. I'm just watching the football.'

'Thank you.'

In the awkward silence that followed, he almost wished she hadn't approached him, since he now felt obliged to try and get information out of her.

'Can I get either of you a drink?' the bartender asked.

'A pint, please. Chloe?'

'I'm fine, thank you.'

'Are you sure? My treat. Oh God.' Chris brought his palm to his face in mock embarrassment. 'I've just fallen into the chatting-up category.'

'Just a small glass of wine then, please.'

While she examined the wine list, Chris cast his eyes around the bar. Was Hannah or one of the other team watching them? But then it struck him that, if they were, Chloe — if it *was* her — would surely have recognised them.

'So, what do you do for a living?' Chloe asked.

'I'm a civil servant. You know, one of those plebs who does all the work while others take the credit for it. How about you?'

'I'm between jobs at the moment, which is why I decided to pay my old friend a surprise visit.'

'I'm guessing it didn't go as planned, since you're here by yourself.'

'No, it didn't. I think it was a bit of a shock. Hopefully, we'll be able to meet up properly tomorrow.'

The bartender handed them their drinks, Chris slipping the receipt into his pocket.

'Cheers,' he said, and they clinked glasses. He decided against trying to get any information out of her. Chloe or not, this would probably be her last evening of peace and quiet before the real interrogation began.

CHAPTER 18

Adam Coulthard
October 2021

I followed her for a while before I finally managed to get her alone.

I ran towards her, calling her name. She didn't even look my way. I guessed she was probably working and was using a false identity. I went up to her and put my hand on her arm, which made her jump.

'It's okay. I know you're working.'

She stared at me. 'Sorry?'

'It's me — Adam.'

'I'm sorry but I don't have a clue who you are.' Her eyes darted around as if she were looking for a way to escape. Up close, I saw her freckles, and the slightly crooked nose that she'd told me she'd broken years ago. It was Chloe all right.

'I know you're working, that you told me I should never approach you when you're out in the field, but—'

'I need to go.' She began to walk away fast.

'They told me you were dead, but I never gave up hope. I did what you told me to and sent that necklace with the weird inscription to Jen.' But Chloe merely increased her pace.

'Chloe, please!' I cried.

'Look, just leave me alone, will you? I'll scream.' She rummaged in her bag and took out a battered mobile phone. 'I'll call the police and tell them someone's bothering me.'

I held up my hand and stepped back. 'Okay, Chloe, I'm sorry. If that's the way you want it . . .' And I walked away.

I couldn't believe she'd just blanked me like that. What was she playing at? I returned home and booted up the computer. I hadn't used it in so long, it took quite a while. The home screen still showed the picture of Chloe and me together, my arm around her. I decided to check social media — everyone has social media, right? If she wasn't Chloe, I'd find her there. I spent the whole night and part of the next morning with my eyes glued to the screen — Instagram, Facebook, Twitter and even LinkedIn, but she was nowhere. I pulled out every photo I owned of Chloe in case I'd been mistaken. I wasn't.

CHAPTER 19

Sean Sterling
November 2021

'You here again, Mr Sterling?' Mabel said.

'Yes, I want to be here when she wakes up — whenever that is.'

'I know you've got a lot on your mind at the moment, but did you manage to find Chloe's NHS number?' the nurse asked.

'No, but I did find our marriage certificate.' Sean produced an envelope from his bag. 'The doctors were asking about Chloe's maiden name.'

'Ah yes, thank you. Mind if I just go and make a copy of it?' Mabel took the certificate from him.

'I don't know how much help it'll be. As I said, we kept our own names when we married.'

'Well, I'll do one anyway and let the doctors decide.'

'And I'll keep searching for that pesky NHS number.'

'Thank you. She's a very lucky lady.'

When the nurse had gone, Sean took hold of his wife's hand and stroked it. 'I really miss you, Chloe. Please come back to me.' A tear fell on to her pale hand. 'I brought some nail polish for you. You always said this was your favourite colour. I'll try and paint your nails for you later, or maybe the nurse will do it for me.'

He couldn't help feeling stupid, but the doctors had said talking to her was a good thing to do and might help speed up her recovery. The rhythmic beep of the machine monitoring her heart rate continued in the background. Sometimes he'd count the beeps between phrases. He sighed. Days were turning into weeks, and still Chloe showed no sign of life. They had told him they couldn't say how long she'd be like this for, or what her mental capacity would be if, or when, she woke up. He kept expecting the doctor to tell him that she was a lost cause and that it was time to turn off the machines. Meanwhile, he kept talking, trying not to lose hope. She'd show them, prove that she was a fighter. She had always been a fighter. She was just resting until it was time to rejoin the battle.

Beep . . . beep . . . beep . . .

CHAPTER 20

Hannah Littlefair
2023

Early the following morning, Hannah knocked at the door to Chris's room. It took several minutes of knocking before he opened up, upon which she marched straight inside.

'What happened to coming up to mine for a debrief last night?' she demanded.

'I was shattered, Han.' Chris trailed after her. 'What time is it anyway?'

'Six a.m.'

'Jeez, I thought I was here to relax.'

'So, come on. I'm waiting. I've been up all night worrying about you,' she said.

'Now I know you're lying.'

'Okay, I was up trying to sort stuff out, but I was thinking about you.'

'Well, it was already late when she asked if she could join me.'

'What? Hang on. She? You sat with the woman you were supposed to be following?' Hannah plonked herself down on the bed. 'You really should have informed me, Chris.'

'Come on, Hannah, I'm not stupid. I'd have told you at once if there was anything worth reporting.'

'So? What happened? What did she say?' Hannah was furious. He seemed to be treating this like it was some game.

'She asked if she could sit with me because she was afraid some drunk businessman would bother her. I could hardly refuse, could I? I bought her a glass of wine.'

Hannah groaned.

'What?' Chris asked.

'Nothing.' Though it was far from being nothing.

'I kept the receipt.' He fished it out of his pocket. 'We chatted, like you do. She said she'd come to Long Eaton to visit a friend as a surprise, but it hadn't gone well.'

Hannah made a face. 'True.'

'She told me she was between jobs at the moment, and asked me what I did. I told her I was a civil servant.'

'That's it? She didn't say anything else, like who she was or where she'd come from?'

'Nope. I watched the footie, she drank her wine, we went our separate ways. End of report, ma'am. I'll have my written statement on your desk by end of day.' Chris wandered over to the window and stood with his back to her. 'So, can I go back to my life now?'

'You don't want to come back to London with me?'

He shook his head. 'Not really.'

'I can't believe you're not as keen as I am to solve this puzzle. Don't you want to find out who she is?' Hannah was surprised by his seeming indifference.

'Please don't drag me into anything this time.' He continued to gaze out of the window as he spoke, his back to her.

'Look,' she said. 'The car is picking me and our mystery guest up at nine a.m. If you want to come along, send Jen a message and she'll arrange to have you picked up. If not, I'll see you next time I'm up.' It sounded so final somehow. Hannah left before he could see her cry.

CHAPTER 21

Jen Garner

They hadn't been driving long before Jen started to get tired of Sam gushing over the kids. 'They're sooo adorable.'

Jen gave a wry smile. 'I wouldn't go that far.'

'Melanie is the total clone of you.'

Jen rolled her eyes. 'I'll take that as a compliment.' She pulled on to the A-road that would take them to Nottingham and the office.

'And Alex! Oh my God. Where do I get one? He's just so cute.'

'Glad to see they made a good impression,' Jen said. 'You do realise it's all an act?'

'Melanie just has your mannerisms down to a T.'

'She's well-rehearsed.'

'They've got me all broody, Jen.'

'Now that isn't a good thing. You should come and stay when they're being a nightmare.' Jen laughed, pleased to be finally pulling into the station car park. 'Anyway, welcome to Nottingham city police.'

'Shall I get out?' Sam asked.

'You'll be fine. The security isn't quite as up to scratch as London's.' Jen found a space and they made for the stairs.

'I just need to pop in and see the team, then we'll head up to the boss's office.'

'I thought Chris was still off work,' Sam said.

'Oh no, this is the number one boss.'

'Ah, I see.' Though Sam sounded doubtful.

* * *

Eyeing the mess in the Superintendent's office, which was overflowing with loose papers and stacks of files, Jen went off to make them all a drink, leaving Sam with the Superintendent. She hoped he and Sam would hit it off. She had faith in Sam's ability to charm whoever she met, and if working out in the field was proving difficult for her, maybe a return to secretarial work would be the best option. Plus, Jen was about to ask him for time off, and she wasn't sure how to broach the subject. She couldn't tell him that she was going back to London and her old team. She'd just have to go with the family emergency angle.

Jen forced a grin as she re-entered his office and noticed that Sam was now sitting at Margaret's old desk. She handed her her drink and, taking a deep breath, knocked on the Superintendent's door.

'Sir, your drink.' Jen walked in and cleared a space amid the scattered files, then placed the steaming mug down.

'So, what can I do for you, Jennifer?' She noted that he'd used her "Sunday" name. Not a good sign.

She got straight to the point. 'Sir, I've come to ask if I could take some leave.'

'When? You've only been in this job, what, three months?'

'With immediate effect, sir.'

'I beg your pardon?' His tone was frosty.

'I'm sorry, sir, but James's mum is critically ill.' The lie slipped so easily off her tongue that she almost convinced herself that her mother-in-law was at death's door. 'We need to get down there before the worst happens.'

'Hmm,' Gil muttered. 'And the girl outside?'

'I thought she'd make a great secretary, boss. She'd have your office sorted in no time at all.'

'So you brought her along to soften the blow.'

'Well, I—'

'Despite what you say, it's clear to me that something is going on. And the arrival of one of your London friends suggests that it has to do with your old job.'

'Sir—'

He held up his hand. 'Let me finish. When you started working with us I distinctly remember telling you that you couldn't chop and change whenever you felt like a bit of action. It's either local policing here — which may not be so exciting — or the service back in London.'

'I know, sir, but—'

'We are short-staffed in the absence of our DI. While things may appear to be—' Gil stopped before he said the words guaranteed to set all the criminals in Nottingham on a looting spree.

'Quiet,' Jen finished for him.

He gave a harrumph. 'Yes, well, if you're telling the truth and James's mother is sick, then of course you must go and pay your respects. However, if word reaches my ear that you've gone back to your old team and are participating in some high-octane adventure, don't bother coming back. Am I making myself understood, Jennifer? I need committed officers in my team, not individuals who disappear when something more exhilarating comes up.'

'Thank you, sir.' Jen got to her feet, hoping that Gil hadn't noticed how flushed her face was. Had she really just been told not to return?

'Tell your friend out there that if she wants the job, it's hers.'

'Will do, sir.' Jen went through to the outer office, where Sam sat waiting for her.

'Everything okay?' Sam asked.

'Well, if you'd like a secretarial job up here in Nottingham, it's yours,' Jen said, and marched off.

Sam hurried out after her. 'Jen, wait. I don't get you. What did you just say?'

'The Superintendent needs a secretary, and since being out in the field isn't going too well for you, I thought—'

'But what will I do about my life in London? My flat? My things?'

'That's the easy bit.' Jen turned to face her. 'I'm going to need somewhere in London to stay, so I'll flat-sit for you.'

'But what about me? Where do I stay until I can find somewhere here?'

'Well, I'm sure James will be more than happy to put you up, since the kids have been scooted off to their grandparents.'

'All because of this Chloe woman appearing?' Sam asked.

'Yeah . . . Hannah and Max decided it was best for them to be removed from the situation, just in case something happened.'

'Do James's parents mind?'

'Na, they love it when they come and stay. Plus, the fresh air of Wetton will do them good.'

'I wouldn't want to put James out though.'

'Alternatively, there are plenty of hotels, or I'm sure one of the team can put you up.'

'They don't know me though.'

'Tell you what. Come back to London with me, Max and Chris later. You can make up your mind about what you want to do on the way.'

'I'm not sure I can just upend my life and move to Nottingham. It's such a big decision to make.'

'Have a think. It's a good couple of hours back to London, and if you decide that being the Superintendent's secretary isn't for you, then fine. As long as you don't mind me crashing with you for a couple of days.'

'Okay.' Sam sounded dubious.

CHAPTER 22

Hannah Littlefair

Hannah stood at the door to the mystery woman's room and listened. Hearing no movement from inside, she knocked loudly.

The woman's muffled voice called out. 'Just a minute.'

Hannah waited, wondering if she should force her way in. She could be doing anything in there. She might even have an accomplice.

The woman opened the door.

'May I come in?' Hannah said.

'Of course.'

'Sleep okay?' Hannah glanced at the bed, which did look as if it had been slept in.

'Yes, thanks. I went and sat in the bar for a bit. When I came back up here I was out like a light as soon as my head hit the pillow. It was nice to sleep in a comfy bed for once.'

'Good. Look, I'm going to be straight with you,' Hannah said. 'The reason we're finding it difficult to believe you are Chloe Seaward is because Chloe was cremated a little over two years ago. She'd been found dead.'

The woman opened her mouth to speak but Hannah raised a hand. 'Let me finish. The fact that you've turned up claiming to be Chloe Seaward puts us in a difficult position—'

'But I *am* Chloe.'

'Then whose was the body we identified as yours?' The woman merely shrugged. 'I would like you to come back to London with me.'

'What do I need to do to prove that what I say is true? Look. I'll show you the damn tattoo.' She bent to roll up her trousers.

'I'm going to ask you to speak to one of our psychologists who will give you a lie detector test,' Hannah continued.

'Okay, fine. Is Lisa coming too?'

'I'm not sure,' Hannah said. 'Why do you ask?'

The woman smiled. 'It would be good to catch up with her again after all this time.'

'I'm going to call for a car,' Hannah said. 'Meet me downstairs in, say, half an hour? Will that give you enough time to get ready?'

'Yeah.'

But Hannah didn't move. 'Look, this is your last chance to walk away. I won't come after you or whoever sent you. Just leave Lisa and her family alone.'

CHAPTER 23

Chloe Seaward

So, this was how they were treating her. She could hardly believe it. Instead of the welcome she'd expected, they'd bundled her into a blacked-out BMW like some criminal about to be tried. She was surprised they hadn't put cuffs on her.

She closed her eyes. Despite telling Hannah she'd slept well, she had spent the whole night wondering what the hell was going on. Had they forgotten about her out in the field? So much so that they'd mixed her up with some dead woman? There was no way this would have happened when Max was in charge.

She had done what they had sent her to do and cleared up the mess they'd left after they arrested Jessica, the daughter of one of the country's biggest drugs lords, who was trying to continue her dad's legacy. How had they missed the reason she was running around a storage facility in the dead of night? Her mistake had been to turn up at Lisa's like she had. But that still didn't justify what they were doing to her now.

Chloe opened her eyes, expecting to see the suburbs of London. But instead of endless streets of houses she saw vast green fields, and not a house in sight. Abruptly, the car turned into a narrow gravel lane. They bumped along it for a few minutes before coming to a halt outside an isolated cottage that hadn't been visible from the road.

Chloe got out of the car. 'What's going on, Hannah?'

'I decided to bring you here rather than taking you to London. It's one of our safe houses,' Hannah said.

Chloe looked around. 'But it's out in the middle of nowhere.'

'It's actually not that far from London. It's very homely; you'll be quite comfortable here.'

'Why not take me back to the office?' Chloe said.

'Because if you are Chloe Seaward and you've been undercover all this time, we need to keep you safe until you're debriefed.'

'Where's Lisa? Isn't she coming?'

'She's staying in Nottingham,' Hannah answered. She led the way to the front door, knocked, and was greeted by a pretty young woman with long blonde hair.

'Morning, ma'am.'

'Elispeth, this is Chloe Seaward. Hopefully you were told to expect her?' Hannah said.

'Yes, I was. Come in.'

Elispeth stepped aside and they went through into a sitting room furnished with worn, comfortable-looking sofas. A large open fire was burning, and Chloe saw neat stacks of wood on either side of the hearth. She went over to it and held out her hands to the warmth. 'It's nice here.'

Hannah smiled. 'Elispeth will be taking care of you while you're here.'

'I will need to get something to wear and a few essentials,' Chloe said.

'You'll find some of your own clothes in the wardrobe in your room, and Elispeth has picked up anything else you might need.'

'Well, er, thanks . . . I guess.'

'We suggest you stay in as much as possible so as to remain out of sight. A doctor will be along later to examine you,' Hannah said.

'What for? I'm fine,' Chloe said.

'It may help us determine your identity,' Hannah continued. 'For all intents and purposes, Chloe Seaward is dead. Dead and buried. We need to find out who you really are, and a physical examination is part of that.'

'So, really, I'm a prisoner here.'

'We have no legal case against you, so you can come and go as you please,' Hannah said.

'But you'll have me followed every step of the way,' Chloe muttered. 'Fine, I'd better find my room then.'

As she headed up the stairs, she heard Elispeth call after her. 'I'll make you a cuppa.'

'Whatever.'

CHAPTER 24

November 2021

The first thing I'm aware of is a rhythmic beeping in the background. I'm almost scared to open my eyes in case there's just more darkness. I feel it calling me back, telling me it's safer and warmer down there in the black, empty pit, but I'm fighting it. I've been asleep too long. I try to move my hand but it won't respond.

A voice keeps repeating someone's name: 'Chloe.' Should I know this Chloe person? I search my memory. I'm terrified to find that I can't remember anything, not even who I am.

Amid the cacophony of voices someone lifts my hand and holds it. The pressure on my wrist somehow causes sensation to return to other parts of my body too. The darkness seems to peel away and I make out coloured shapes floating above me. I blink. Why can't I see anything clearly? Then I am struck by the most intense pain. My brain feels like it's trying to escape, ramming the inside of my skull. I hear that voice again, more clearly now: 'Chloe.'

'Chloe, everything is okay. You're in hospital, your husband is here. You're going to be okay.'

I try to speak, but there's a tube down my throat. I want to ask who Chloe is, why I am here, but I can't make a sound. Like a fish, my

58

mouth opens and closes wordlessly. Something cool and narrow touches my lips. 'Suck, Chloe.' A jet of cold liquid fills my mouth and my throat contracts. I swallow. Bliss.

'Oh my God, Chloe, I've been so worried.' There is a weight on the bed next to me, a dark shape.

'It might take some time for her to speak again.' The words seem to come from one of the shapes moving in front of my eyes.

'I'm just so happy that Chloe is back with us again.' None of this is making any sense and I can't speak to ask them what is going on. The pain in my head is making it impossible to think. Suddenly, it is all too much. I close my eyes and wait for the blessed abyss to engulf me.

'Chloe! Oh my God! What's happening?'

'Sean, she's fine. She's just begun to awaken. Understandably, it's tired her out and she's fallen asleep.'

'Does that mean she's gone back into a coma again?'

'No, not at all, Sean. We just need to be patient. With time she'll regain full consciousness. Right now, her brain is still in the process of repairing itself after the trauma she suffered. I think we can at least get this ventilator removed. I'll just go and find a doctor.'

CHAPTER 25

Hannah Littlefair
2023

As Hannah left the cottage, Elispeth whispered, 'Are you sure
that's not Chloe?' As if she hadn't been asking herself this very
question ever since the woman turned up. She had left it up
to Elispeth to decide how she wanted to play it — whether or
not she treated her like Chloe. She only told Elispeth never to
call Jen Garner by her real name, and must instead always refer
to her as Lisa Carter, though she could mention James. She
wasn't to prevent their guest from going out, since Hannah
had placed a team on watch, ready to move at a moment's
notice if she strayed too far. They would barge in if anyone
unknown to them intruded.

     Hannah got into the car, telling the driver to take her to
the office. As they drove, she stared out of the window, trying
to work out what to do next. There was no protocol for when
a dead person suddenly came back to life. Most troubling of all
was how the woman kept referring to things from the past that
only Chloe should have known. The thoughts whirling about
her head made it feel as if it were about to explode. What she

needed was someone to unload on — Chris, in other words. Though he had enough on his plate already, what with his MS diagnosis.

* * *

Reminding herself to smile, she strode, heels clicking, past the row of desks, hoping none of the team would ask her about the woman now ensconced in the safe house. Fat chance of that.

'Is it true?'

'Did the special ops team in Nottingham get it wrong?'

'Our guys saw the results of the autopsy; how come they got it so wrong?'

'And all the stuff with Lisa. It makes even less sense now.'

'Chill, guys.' Hannah made an attempt to smile. 'The old gossip mill keeps on turning, doesn't it? Whoever's interested can come to the main meeting room in thirty minutes for a briefing. Bring your notebooks, and if any of you has something strong hidden in their bottom drawer, now's the time to bring it out. Extra brownie points for chocolate.'

Hannah unlocked her office door, went inside and collapsed on the sofa. God, what a tangled web this was. And, as always, Jennifer Garner sat like a fat spider right at the heart of it.

* * *

'Hmm. I see we have a full house. I don't think I've ever seen the meeting room this busy. Keep it up and we'll have to ask for a bigger one.' From hand to hand a plastic beaker was passed to her, smelling suspiciously like whisky. 'I won't ask where this came from.' Hannah downed it in one, relishing the burn.

'So, to business,' she said. 'As you obviously all know, at around seven p.m. yesterday evening a woman turned up on Jennifer Garner's doorstep claiming to be Chloe Seaward, who, as you also all know, is supposedly dead.' A low rumble of voices ran around the room. 'The unknown woman has been temporarily placed in one of our safe houses — in Houghton, to be precise — under the watchful eye of Detective Dixon.'

'So, what happens now?' Tim asked.

'In my opinion, we need to look into where she was before she went to Jen's. Georgina — get on the CCTV, see if we can trace her movements leading up to her reappearance. I have already asked a doctor to come and assess our mystery woman and perform a lie detector test. Chloe had at least one tattoo — which she showed to Jen — and a number of other scars. It will be an easy matter to compare them. I want to look at that boyfriend again — Adam Coulthard. Jen should be here soon; she can go and see him and hear what he has to say for himself.'

'What about exhuming Chloe's body?' a voice called from the back of the room.

'Cremated,' came the answer. 'I will of course interview our mystery woman after she's been left to stew for a while. Fingerprints and DNA are the silver bullets in this case.'

'Why not just leave her waiting while we run a DNA test?' the same person called out.

'As we all know, DNA results can take forty-eight to seventy-two hours to come back — if there's no backlog. We can't afford to sit on our arses until then. If this isn't Chloe, who knows what they have planned. And how does she know so much about our past cases? About Jen? On the other hand, if she *is* Chloe, where did we go so wrong?'

'That's easily blamed on the Nottingham team, isn't it?' Tim said.

Hannah ignored his comment.

'Does this case take precedence over our other investigations?' someone wanted to know.

'We mustn't give criminals a free pass because we've got issues of our own to be worrying about. I'll look at the workload before assigning any tasks. Jen is on her way down, along with Chris, and I'm sure they will be keen to assist.'

'Sam not returning, then?' somebody asked.

'I'm not sure about that. I guess we'll find out when the car gets here later.' Hannah cast her eyes around the room. 'And, please, I want Chloe's reappearance to remain between these four walls. Finally, if she's brought here at any point, watch how you refer to Jen, because the woman thinks she's Lisa Carter.'

'Maybe it would be best if we just all refer to Jen as Lisa?' Tim suggested.

'Yes, I think that's a good idea, just to be on the safe side. Right. Any further questions?'

'If this *is* Chloe,' Tim continued, 'shouldn't we at least send someone up to Nottingham to see how they managed to cock it up?'

'Detective, that is not the right attitude. We are one force, and we don't shove the blame on to another team when it suits us. We worked together on the case, if you remember.'

'Yes, but we didn't identify her, did we? We just went with what the Nottingham pathologist told us,' Tim countered.

'We are not getting embroiled in a blame game. All right?'

CHAPTER 26

Chloe Seaward

Hearing the detective on the phone, Chloe went to her room and ransacked the wardrobe. To her surprise, she found her old clothes, just as Hannah had said. Even more surprising was that they still fitted her, although the jeans were a bit tight. Maybe once they'd got this stupid problem of her identity cleared up, she'd treat herself to a whole new get-up. She certainly deserved it.

Showered and changed, she came downstairs. 'So, what's there to do around here, since they said I'm not being kept prisoner?'

'I think they want you to stay close, to be honest,' Elispeth said.

So, I am a prisoner. Thought so.

Chloe's suspicion must've been apparent on her face, for the younger woman hastened to add, 'Only because they are concerned for your safety, what with you being undercover for so long.'

'Can I at least go out into the garden?' Chloe asked.

'Of course. I'll make us some drinks and we can sit and enjoy the sunshine.'

Chloe laughed bitterly. 'We can play spot the security patrol.'

'Yeah, like *Where's Wally?*' Elispeth said.

'I used to love those books when I was younger.' Chloe caught herself actually smiling. 'I wasn't exactly paying attention earlier — what was your name again?'

'Elispeth. Detective Elispeth Dixon.'

'Well, despite what they say, I'm Chloe Seaward.' Her voice was defiant.

'Let's hope we're not stuck here for too long,' Elispeth said.

'Yeah. If only that DNA swab doesn't take an age.'

Sensing Chloe's frustration building again, the younger woman clapped her hands together. 'Right. Tea? Or do you fancy something cold?'

'Tea'll be good, thanks.' Chloe stepped out into the garden, which was surprisingly tidy. It even had a patio with table and chairs. This certainly wasn't like the other safe houses she'd been in. With a quick look around the garden to see if she could spot any of the watchers, she settled into a seat and turned her face up to the sun. God, she needed this.

'Here you go, hun.' Elispeth appeared, bearing a tray of drinks. 'You spotted anyone yet?'

'No, but I wasn't looking. I had my eyes closed, enjoying the sun,' Chloe said.

'Go for it. I've brought my sewing, so you just sit back and relax.'

A comfortable silence fell between the two women for a time, until Chloe broke it suddenly. 'What's Hannah like as a boss? I remember the day she joined — all eager and excited.'

'She's pretty cool. When she first took over she was a bit overwhelmed, but I guess I would be too in her place. Not only the heavy-duty crime she has to deal with but those meetings with the government. It's a lot to take on.'

'I just wish I'd known that Max was retiring, I'd have come back sooner. That job was supposed to be mine.' Chloe let out a short laugh. It wasn't that she was jealous of Hannah, but finding a job she'd been promised already taken, well, it was a bit hard to accept.

'Hmmm.' Elispeth was clearly being noncommittal.

'Okay, I know you guys all thought I was dead . . .' Chloe's voice trailed off.

'Can I ask why you stopped checking in with your handler? I mean, at least they'd have known you were still out there then.'

'Here we go. Straight in with the interview questions. You've been spending too much time with Lisa,' Chloe said.

'God, I wish. Lisa was the stuff of legend,' Elispeth said.

'Why has Lisa come back? I thought she was all happily settled in domesticity.'

Elispeth gave her a sideways glance. 'She came back to investigate Chloe Seaward's death.'

'Ah, okay. At least she managed to stop the drugs before she left, and take Jessica out of the equation.'

'I never had anything to do with her, but she sounds like a pretty nasty piece of work.'

Chloe nodded grimly. 'Jessica was into everything. It's just a shame Dana had to die for them to close the paedophile ring.'

'Yeah, Lisa came back for that investigation too,' Elispeth said.

'Bet Lisa's regretting having left.'

'Oh, I don't know. I'd leave for love — I think. After all, love is just a fairy tale invented to keep us in our place, isn't it? Riding off into the sunset and all that shit—'

'Gee, that would be nice.' Chloe laughed.

'So, come on. Between us two, where *have* you been for the last two years?' Elispeth asked.

'Clearing up the mess you guys left,' Chloe muttered.

Elispeth's sewing lay untouched on her lap. 'Were you around when Lisa first left?'

'No, I started — what, three-ish years ago? It was a bad time.' Chloe sighed. 'She'd gone off to find her happily ever after, and Max wasn't his normal self. I'd lost my best friend, so I threw myself into work. We thought we'd picked everyone up when George Crawford went down, but somehow we missed his daughter Jessica—'

'I didn't think they knew each other,' Elispeth commented.

'They didn't, but Jessica was already making a name for herself as a criminal, and once she found out who her real dad was — not to mention the drug empire he'd built up — well, there was no stopping her.'

'So, how did you find out about Jessica?'

'At first I was tucked up in the office, but after a bit I started to go out. I took risks. I guess I went a bit wild, and that's how I came across Jessica. It took a lot of work to get close to Jess, but when I did — shit, that girl was something else.' Chloe shook her head.

'So why not come back in and tell Max what they'd missed?' Elispeth asked.

'I wanted to make sure I had everything this time, so I started going to her sex parties. I slept with people from the monarchy, government and other important public figures who should have known better. I wanted them all to pay for the suffering they were causing, to people like Mikel, who had been at the centre of the paedophile ring, for crying out loud — people who had done nothing.' Chloe hated to think of what she'd been a part of back then, but she knew why she'd acted as she had. Through it all, she had always kept to her principles.

Elispeth was silent for a while. 'I read some of the case files. It was all pretty horrific.'

'As to why I stopped checking in, it was simple,' Chloe continued. 'I hated my handler. I didn't trust him at all. I needed to go in alone, knowing that what I was getting into was dangerous.'

Elispeth stared at her. 'I'm in awe.'

'And look where it's all got me,' Chloe murmured. Then she roused herself. 'I don't suppose I could use your mobile phone for a second, could I?'

Elispeth shook her head. 'I'm really sorry, Chloe, but . . .'

'It's fine, I shouldn't have asked. You've been so nice to me. I shouldn't take advantage.'

'It's just that Hannah said—'

Chloe held up a hand. 'Forget I asked.'

'Is there something I can look up for you? I can't let you use my phone, but if you tell me what you're looking for—'

'No, it's good. Thank you. It can wait.' Chloe changed the subject. 'What time's this shrink supposed to be coming?'

'Around five, I think,' Elispeth said.

'Good. Plenty of time to sit and soak up the sun.' Chloe sat back and closed her eyes.

CHAPTER 27

Jen Garner

'Jen. Max. Welcome.' Hannah kissed each of them on the cheek. 'Chris not coming then?'

'No, he said he was going to get the Tube back to yours,' Jen said.

'Oh. Right.'

'I don't think it's anything to worry about,' Jen continued. 'I expect he's just tired, what with all the excitement over Chloe's sudden reappearance.'

'It's just that I gave him quite an earful this morning. I hope he isn't brooding.'

'He was pretty quiet on the way down,' Max said.

Hannah turned to him. 'I expect you'll be wanting me out of your office now you're back. I should warn you, I've made a few changes.'

'No, you're still the boss. I just needed to know if . . .' He shrugged.

'I've just arranged for a DNA sample to be taken. We'll know for sure when the results come back,' Hannah said.

Recalling the DNA tests on the dead woman, Jen wondered if it really was that simple. 'And in the meantime?'

'Well, I want to interview her myself for a start,' Hannah replied.

'Wouldn't it be better if someone who didn't know Chloe questioned her?' Jen asked.

Hannah frowned. 'Like who?'

'I don't know — Tim? I just think she might pick up hints from our body language. Plus, we have formed an opinion of Chloe, so we're biased. What about the DI?'

'She's met him,' Hannah said. 'I had him watch her while we were at the hotel.'

'There must be someone in this department who never knew Chloe,' Jen persisted, 'and who was unaffected by her death.'

Max nodded. 'I think Jen's right, Hannah.'

Hannah pondered the suggestion. 'I could really do with Sam right now.'

'Yeah, about that,' Jen said. 'I think I've got her a job up in Nottingham. Since you were saying she's struggling with undercover work and the Superintendent's secretary has just retired, I thought—'

'She'd be better off doing what she knows best.' Hannah smiled. 'You're probably right.'

'She's back in London, though. She came back in the car with us. We dropped her off at her flat to get some stuff together — that is, if she decides to leave.' Jen looked a bit sheepish. 'I think I kinda sprung the idea on her, but I needed to leave the Superintendent something positive in return for my sudden request for time off.'

Hannah eyed Jen shrewdly. 'What reason did you give him?'

'She told him that James's mother was seriously ill,' Max said.

'And then the Super told me that if I was coming to join you guys in some high-octane action, then I shouldn't bother going back.' Jen made a wry face.

'What are you doing here then?' Hannah demanded. 'You're not indispensable, you know. We can crack this without you.'

'That's what I said,' Max added.

'I need to know what happened to my best friend,' Jen almost wailed. 'That's why I came back.'

'Well, if that's how it is, you and Chris can go and see Adam Coulthard,' Hannah said.

Jen did a small double take. 'Now there's someone I've not thought about in a while.'

'If this woman is Chloe, why didn't she go back to him?' Hannah wondered aloud. 'Weren't they all set to marry?'

'Yeah, why come to mine if the love of your life is waiting for you at home?' Jen added.

'He'd be the first person I'd want to see if I was in her shoes. She's been gone for, what, two years? More?' Hannah said.

It was Jen's turn to nod. 'I guess me and the DI are off to Reading first thing, then.'

'What do you need me to do, Hannah?' Max said. 'You're in charge now, this is your show. I'm just here to help.'

'Desk in the corner be okay?' Hannah giggled as Max scanned the room. 'I've got a pile of reports that need typing up.'

Finally, Max got it. 'Boss to secretary in under a year. I must be the first person to be demoted that fast.'

'You can make yourself at home in the meeting room,' Hannah said.

'Meeting room it is then.'

CHAPTER 28

November 2021

It's that damn beeping again, cutting through the comfortable darkness and bringing me back. What will I find this time? More coloured shapes? More pain? I hear voices.

'The indications are positive, Mr Sterling. We've seen an increase in your wife's brain activity.'

'Does that mean she's going to be okay? Fully recover, I mean.'

'I'm afraid we're going to have to wait a little longer for that.'

I open my eyes. Things are clearer now. Instead of indistinct shapes, there are people's faces. I wonder who they are. I try to speak, but the words still refuse to form. I want to ask where I am, who they are, and what happened to bring me here. At least my brain has stopped crashing against my skull. It's just a nagging pain now.

Suddenly I am dazzled. A light in my eye, and behind it a face, close yet blurry. They are still repeating that name. Maybe it's me.

'Chloe . . .'

I can't move my limbs. Why can't I move them? I'm not tied down. Why can't I speak? I'm not gagged. Above me, they continue to talk, their voices muffled, as if they're underwater. Perhaps I'm drowning, something pulling me down to the depths.

CHAPTER 29

Adam Coulthard
October 2021

I returned to Chessington the following day and booked myself into a hotel in case she didn't appear and I had to stay longer. I was determined to confront Chloe and ask her why she was pretending not to know me. The service must have done something to her. Maybe they'd wiped me from her memory because I wasn't suitable. Maybe that was why they told me she was dead.

It wasn't long before I caught sight of her again. In the middle of the day, at around lunchtime, I saw her hurrying across the marketplace. This time I didn't approach her. Instead, I followed her from place to place — the supermarket, the library. I followed her home, an anonymous high-rise on the outskirts of Chessington. Exactly the sort of place I expected an agent from the service to live in.

I couldn't follow her into the building — she would have seen me — so once she'd disappeared through the main outer door, I'd lost her. I could follow one of the residents into the building, but how on earth was I going to find out which of

73

the 127 flats was hers? I decided to spend the night outside, watching, in case she went out. That happened sooner than I'd expected. At about 11 p.m. she left the building again, heading to the refuse area with a bag of rubbish. This was my chance; the area was deserted.

'Chloe?' I approached her slowly, my hands in the air. She made as if she hadn't seen me, so I tried again.

'Chloe?'

She jumped. 'You again.'

'Chloe, you don't need to pretend anymore, there's no one to hear. I know it's you.'

'Look, I have no idea who this Chloe person is, or who you are.' She turned to walk away.

Why did she keep saying she doesn't know who I am? Angry now, I grabbed her by the arms and shook her violently.

'What have they done to you? Why won't you acknowledge me?'

'Please! Please, stop.' She started to cry. 'I'll be whoever you say, just stop.' I dropped her arms and stepped back. What had I done? This was the woman I loved more than anything in the world, and I was doing her harm.

'Oh God. Chloe, I'm so sorry.' But she was gone. She ran towards a black Fiesta, fumbled in her pocket and tried the doors, then sprinted back towards the building. I just stood, watching her, wretched. Not wanting to frighten her more than I already had, I made my way back to the hotel and drank myself into oblivion.

CHAPTER 30

DI Chris Jackson
2023

Chris unlocked the door to Hannah's flat and stepped inside. Every time he came here it gave him a shock. The place was a shit-tip: clothes piled on chairs, bits of make-up scattered across the tables, tangles of charge cables attached to various sockets. His cleaners would have a fit. How she ever managed to find anything in the chaos was beyond him. No wonder Hannah never invited anyone round. Chris wondered if she would move into Max's old place, or whether they had somewhere else lined up for her now she was the boss. In her new position she'd need somewhere with a bit more security. No point trying to tidy it for her; she would only be annoyed because he'd moved stuff and she couldn't find anything. He decided to make himself a coffee and sit for a while. The journey had been exhausting. First there was the awkwardness of having to sit with the others. Then there was having to navigate the crowds in the Underground with a walking stick. Maybe he should invest in one that folded up; the NHS one he'd been given was heavy and kept getting in the way. Maybe the tech department could make him one that opened out at the press of a button, like a James Bond weapon.

He took a carton of milk from the fridge and smelled it. It was surprisingly fresh. He was filling the kettle when Hannah's message came through.

Hey, how come you didn't come into the office?

Didn't think you'd want me there, he responded. Though really he was just too tired. He needed to get his head around the implications of Chloe Seaward not being dead, because if she was alive, his team had royally cocked up. Most likely someone in Hannah's office was already putting the blame on the Nottingham street-level cops. Street-level cop. How many times had Max or Hannah accused him of acting like one? So what? There was nothing wrong with being out on the streets. In fact, some of his happiest days had been spent there. Now, thanks to his diagnosis, things were going to have to change.

CHAPTER 31

Hannah Littlefair

Elispeth answered Hannah's call on the first ring. 'All good here. I had a chat with her this afternoon, and as far as I can see, she is totally convinced she's Chloe Seaward.'

'I'm trusting you on this one,' Hannah said. 'Play it as you see fit. A team is in position around the cottage and the cameras are picking up everything inside. If you need help, or there's a problem, all you need do is shout.'

'Thanks, Hannah. I'll report back once she's in bed.'

'Did you get her to give you a DNA sample?' Hannah asked.

'Yes. It should be on its way to the lab now.'

'Brilliant, thank you, Elispeth. Stay safe,' Hannah ended the call. Despite the backup around the cottage, her detective was essentially alone, and Hannah was concerned about her.

She went to speak to her team. 'Elliot, make sure you keep your eyes on the feed from that cottage.'

'Yes, boss.'

'We have an unarmed detective in there with an imposter. At the slightest hint of anything untoward, I want backup in there immediately.'

'Yes, boss. I'm rotating with Ashley so we're both on the ball.'

'Great.' Hannah surveyed the room. 'Where are we with the CCTV?'

Georgina's head appeared above her screen. 'I'm looking at it now.'

'Anything?'

'Not really. I've seen her getting off the train at Long Eaton and I'm trying to track her back from there.'

'Thank you, Georgina. Anyone got anything for me? Preferably something positive.'

'I've requested the files from Chloe's original autopsy,' Tim called out. Annoyed, Hannah didn't respond. She'd made it perfectly clear that they weren't about to start playing the blame game.

'Dr Spellbound is on his way to the safe house to assess our guest. He'll conduct the lie detector test while he's there,' Georgina said.

Hannah thanked her. She was on her way to the meeting room to put Jen and Max in the picture when a detective hurried up to her.

'Hannah,' he panted. 'Kristoff is back. He's just cleared customs.'

'How the hell did he get back into the country?' she demanded. Fuck. Just what she needed. A high-profile criminal back in the country, on top of the Chloe business.

'I don't know, boss. I've just had a call from the airport.'

Not wishing her team to know how badly this news had thrown her, Hannah continued into the meeting room.

'Max, can I see you in my office for a moment?' she said.

'Of course.' He followed her inside and she closed the door behind them.

'Max, I've got a problem and I need your help.'

'What's up?' he said.

'Months back, MI5 were tracking what they thought was a terrorist, and when it turned out he wasn't as big a risk as they thought, they asked us to keep an eye on him. Well, he's just arrived back in the country. Meanwhile, there's this mystery woman in a safe house in Houghton, and I don't know what to do.'

'Hannah, I'm sorry to land this on you now, but I've made up my mind. I'm going home, back into retirement. I'm just too old and tired for this game.'

'What?' Hannah felt her stomach drop. 'You mean you're abandoning me, just when I need you? What happened to "I'm just here to help"?'

'Hannah, I have every faith in you, or I wouldn't have put you forward for the job. If I stay, you'll be forever wanting my approval and checking that you're doing the right thing. You've got a great team here to support you — use them. Plus, I'm tired and too old for all this excitement. I prefer my allotment and book club.'

'So I have to figure it out for myself, have I?'

Max smiled disarmingly.

'You're leaving now? This minute?' He nodded. 'You're telling Jen though?'

'She already knows.'

Hannah sighed. 'So you're just going to slip away?'

Max gave her a quick hug and went to the door. 'Don't forget, you've got a damn fine detective inspector sitting in your flat. What's more, the great Lisa Carter has put her job on the line in order to be here. If you want someone to lean on, who better than them?'

CHAPTER 32

Jen Garner

Max returned to the meeting room. 'How did she take it?' Jen asked.

He shrugged. 'As you'd expect.'

'You could always change your mind.'

'I'm too old for this, Jen. Why do you think I retired in the first place?'

'Back to gardening and the book club then,' she said.

'Yep.' He paused. 'Go easy on Hannah if you can.'

'Meaning?'

'I think she's just beginning to appreciate the size of what she's taken on,' he said.

Jen nodded. 'Noted. You will keep in touch, won't you?'

'Of course. Stay safe, Detective Garner.' With that, Max turned and left.

Thinking that Hannah might need some support, Jen went to her office. 'You okay, Hannah?'

'I think so,' Hannah said. 'Considering that Max has just run off like he's escaping from a burning building.'

'You've managed so far without him.' Jen seated herself on the sofa.

'It was fine while I had one case at a time. I was swimming along nicely. Now, not only do I have Chloe back, but Kristoff is back too. And I've left my boyfriend in my flat, which is a total mess.'

'What's the deal with this Kristoff anyway?' Jen asked.

'Mainly drugs and prostitution. He spends most of his time in Spain where he has a villa.'

'Nice.'

'It looks like there's been a breakdown in intelligence somewhere, seeing as last we heard he was in South America.'

Jen laughed. 'Maybe he came here for the weather. Anyway, you've got more to worry about than some major criminal if Chris finds something he shouldn't in your flat.'

Hannah primmed up her mouth. 'I've nothing to hide from him.'

Jen smiled. 'He *is* a detective, Hannah. He won't be able to stop himself doing a bit of snooping.'

'Chris and I tell each other everything,' Hannah insisted.

He hadn't told her about his diagnosis, though, had he? Jen left the thought unsaid. She herself hadn't properly spoken with Chris since the time they'd been stuck in a lift together, so they still hadn't cleared the air between them.

'Jen?'

'Sorry, Hannah, I was just thinking about tomorrow.'

'I was asking if you'd be willing to help us with this investigation,' Hannah said.

'What? The Kristoff case?' Jen asked.

'You really weren't listening, were you? I want you to take over the Chloe case.'

'The Chloe case?' Jen echoed. She had assumed Hannah would want that one.

'I can't work two cases at once,' Hannah said. Clearly giving Jen Chloe rather than Kristoff needed no explanation.

Jen fought to contain the delight in her voice. 'Of course I'll help you out, Hannah.'

'I'm sure Chris will be happy to lend a hand.' She looked at Jen. 'Everything's okay between you two, isn't it?'

'Yeah, of course.' Jen tried to sound convincing. 'Why wouldn't it be?'

CHAPTER 33

Chloe Seaward

Hearing Elispeth open the door to the doctor, Chloe decided she'd better go and say hello.

Having assumed that they would send a woman, Chloe was slightly surprised to be shaking the hand of a man. Elispeth introduced him as Dr Spellbound.

'Right, Ms Seaward. Okay if we hold the examination in here?' he asked.

She shrugged. 'Sure. Wherever.'

'Good. Now, before we start, let me reassure you that the assessment will be completely confidential. I've asked the team in London to stop recording during the interview.' Of course. Why hadn't it crossed her mind that they'd have cameras in here? She cast her eyes around the room, trying to spot them.

'Detective Dixon will also make herself scarce, so she won't overhear what you say.'

'Okay.'

Elispeth brought a pot of tea and two mugs before withdrawing. Chloe heard the front door open and close.

'Cameras off, please,' Dr Spellbound announced. 'You seem a little concerned, Ms Seaward. Are you okay to begin?'

'I'm good.'

'How are you finding being back?' he asked.

'Back where?'

'Well, I've been told that you've been out of touch, and that for the past two years you've been presumed dead.'

She rolled her eyes. 'A whole bunch of fun.'

'Not quite the welcome you were expecting then?'

'No, although . . .'

'What?'

'Well, they *have* made an effort to make me comfortable. Elispeth seems nice, and they put me up in a hotel before bringing me here, so I guess it could be worse,' Chloe said.

Dr Spellbound raised an eyebrow. 'What do you mean by worse?'

'Well, for a start that Hannah Littlefair doesn't believe I'm Chloe Seaward. She could've had me locked up in the cells till they were certain of my identity.'

'Nevertheless, you haven't felt welcomed,' he said.

'No, I haven't. Even my best friend didn't want to see me,' she grumbled.

He scribbled something in his notepad. 'Do you have somewhere to stay? I mean, if you were to leave here tomorrow, where would you go?'

She shrugged again. 'I guess I'd find somewhere — you know, rent a flat or something.'

'No one special waiting for you?' he asked.

'If that was the case, I wouldn't have gone to Lisa, would I?' she said.

'I sense you're regretting your decision to come back.'

'If I'd known they had considered me dead, I wouldn't have come back at all. I could have gone anywhere in the world and started my life afresh.'

'Where would you have gone?' He regarded her with genuine curiosity.

'You know what? I'd go to Disneyland. Lisa and I were always going to go there — before James, that was.'

At this, the doctor couldn't hide the intrigue from his face. 'Did James coming on the scene change things between you and Lisa?'

'As soon as I saw them together, I knew I was about to lose her.'

'The way you put it makes it sound as though you and she were more than just friends,' he said.

She pondered the statement. She'd never seen it that way before. 'Well, Lisa and I had a different kind of love. We were wild together. James tamed her — she wasn't the same after he came along.'

'Right. Let's turn to the last two years, shall we?'

She sighed. 'I knew this was coming.'

'Why did you wait so long before you came back? Surely after Jessica had been caught there was no longer any threat to your life?'

'They had one job to do, just one, and they still managed to get it wrong,' she said.

'What do you mean?' he asked.

'I had more or less handed Jessica to them on a plate, and they got the wrong fucking day!'

'But if you'd returned to the service, you could have told them that.'

'Once they had Jessica locked up — missing the real reason she was at London Gateway — I decided I'd better check they hadn't overlooked anything else. Then once the coast was clear, I tried to come back, only to find that they'd forgotten all about me.'

'They thought you were dead, so it was to be expected, wasn't it?' he reasoned.

Maybe she should have come back sooner, but she'd been working alone for so long by then that she saw no reason to change. This was all getting too difficult.

'I'd like to take a break,' she said.

Dr Spellbound nodded. 'Yes, we've been talking for a while. Let's have a drink and some fresh air and then we'll get the ball rolling on the medical examination and the lie detector test.'

CHAPTER 34

November 2021

I feel like I am trapped in an endless cycle — rising to the surface and plunging back under. Whenever I wake, the same people are there, hovering above me. I wish I could speak. At least the sensation is returning to my limbs. I can't move much except for my toes but my feet react when they test my reflexes. Whoever decided that the best way to do this was by sticking a pin into your foot must have been a sadist.

There is one person who is not a nurse or a doctor, yet who is always there. He kisses my forehead when I wake up, and I drift into unconsciousness with his hand in mine. He must be someone who is significant to me, but who? My periods of consciousness seem to be growing longer. It can only be a matter of time before I find my voice again. Then I can ask him who he is. Who am I?

CHAPTER 35

Jen Garner

'Honey, I'm home!' Jen called.

Sam opened the door for her. 'Busy day?' she asked.

'I don't know. It's all a bit chaotic at the moment. No one seems to know what to do with this woman.'

Sam ushered her into the sitting room. Jen stood in the doorway, gazing around. 'Wow, this is something else!' Sam had decorated her flat in vivid colours. The furniture was all oak, and the open-plan kitchen had been painted a glossy black.

'Thanks. It does look a bit different from when I first moved in.'

'You've done an amazing job, Sam. I'm almost scared to touch anything in case I break it.'

'Well, I'm sure you'll get used to it after you've been here a while,' Sam said.

'You've decided then?' Jen smiled.

'I think I'll give it a go. What's the worst that can happen, right?'

'The office is pretty full on at the moment anyway,' Jen said.

'Am I needed here? Oh God, I didn't even think about the team.' Sam looked aghast.

'Hun, you need to start thinking about yourself and what's best for *you*. Forget about what's going on here. If I remember rightly, you were a pretty hot secretary.'

Sam laughed. 'Your superintendent did sound pretty desperate.'

'Hmm.'

'Will you be okay here on your own?' Sam asked. 'Sure you don't mind flat-sitting for me?'

Jen waved her hand dismissively. 'Not at all. You're doing me a favour.'

'What about Max? Where is he going to stay?'

'Max has gone back home,' Jen said.

Sam looked baffled. 'What was the point of him coming all the way back here then?'

'I think he only realised when he got here that he should let Hannah get on with it by herself. With him here, she'd always be looking to him for guidance.'

'How did she take it?'

'In all honesty, I don't know. I kinda feel guilty for not talking to her about it,' Jen said. Was she neglecting her role as a friend? But Hannah had Chris to talk to, although knowing Hannah . . . 'I'll send her a message later. Anyway, are you heading off to Nottingham right now?'

'Yes,' Sam said. 'I've booked a room in a hotel.'

'I'm sure someone from Chris's team will hook you up with somewhere. Or there is always mine.'

'Thanks, Jen.' Sam hugged her.

Jen beamed. 'Go and be amazing, Sam.'

'I'll try my best.' Sam picked up her wheelie case and headed for the door. 'Try not to wreck the place.'

Jen gave an exaggerated roll of her eyes. 'As if I would.'

'Oh, and don't forget to feed the cat,' Sam said.

'The cat?' Jen was horrified. Sam hadn't told her there was a cat involved.

Sam burst out laughing. 'You should see your face. Don't worry, I was just having you on.'

CHAPTER 36

Chloe Seaward

Dr Spellbound had clearly been eyeing the level of liquid in Chloe's mug, as no sooner had she placed the empty cup down than he said, 'Ready to start again?'

'I think so. Did you want a cup of tea? Sorry, I never thought to offer.'

'No, I'm fine, thank you.' He reached into his bag and pulled out a bottle of Dr Pepper. She smiled. *Odd choice of drink for a doctor.*

'I'm just going to check your reflexes,' he said.

Chloe's leg jerked as the doctor tapped her knee. 'This always makes me giggle.'

'Right. Height and weight and then we're done.'

'Well, I can answer the height one for you,' she said. 'I've no idea what I weigh now.'

'It's fine, I'll do it.' He rummaged around in his bag. Chloe was amused at the amount of stuff he kept in there, rather like Mary Poppins.

'You carrying scales too?' Chloe asked. 'That bag must weigh a tonne.'

He smiled. 'Elispeth brought them in from the car when I arrived.'

He fussed around, attaching various wires to different parts of her body, taking readings on a machine that beeped. She wondered what they all meant; she'd have to look it up later — if she ever got access to the internet again.

Weight and height recorded, they proceeded to the lie detector test. He explained that the machine would register her blood pressure and resting heart rate. 'Happy to continue?' he asked.

She emitted a glum chuckle. 'It's not like I can say no, is it?'

'The choice is yours. Though of course, if you refuse, they will wonder why.'

'Oh, go on. I just want all this over with so I can go back to being me.'

'Okay. I'm going to ask you a series of ten questions. All you need to do is answer yes or no.'

'And this machine will tell you if I'm lying or not?'

'Yes, basically. I will compare your responses to the readings recorded on the monitors. Ready?'

'As I'll ever be.' She watched nervously as the needle on the machine started to waver.

'Is your name Chloe Seaward?'

'Yes.'

'Do you have blonde hair?'

'Yes.'

'Are your eyes blue?'

'Yes.'

'Do you have a tattoo on your left ankle?'

'Yes.'

'Are you in a relationship?'

'No.'

'Have you ever taken legal drugs?'

'Yes.'

'Do you know a Jen Garner?'

'No.'

'Do you work for the police?'

'Yes.'

'Were you born in 1984?'

'Yes.'

'Do you know anyone called Adam Coulthard?'

'No.'

'Thank you, Chloe.' Dr Spellbound began detaching the various wires.

'Is that it? Just these ten questions will determine my fate?'

'That's right,' he said.

'So? Did I pass?' she asked.

'I'm afraid I can't tell you until I've looked at the recordings.'

'And the earlier assessment?'

'Well, you are perfectly sane, if that helps.'

'Loads.' She poured the remnants of the now lukewarm tea into her mug and took a gulp.

'So—' he finished his own dregs of Dr Pepper before continuing — 'what will you do with yourself for the rest of the day?'

'I might see if I'm allowed to go for a wander later. I can take my minder with me so I don't try to make a run for it.' Laughing, she recalled all the times she'd been escorted by gang members. Now she was on the other side of the fence.

CHAPTER 37

DI Chris Jackson

'I want you, Detective.' She was back. He recognised her smell, felt the weight of her.

'Han.' He spoke without opening his eyes.

'Shhh.' Slowly, she unfastened his trousers and lowered her head . . .

* * *

Chris woke amid pitch blackness to find the bed beside him empty. He had a thumping headache and a raging thirst. The distant sound of someone tapping on a keyboard reached him from the kitchen below. He struggled from the bed and made his unsteady way downstairs. Hannah was at the kitchen table, glasses on, her hair in a messy bun, typing away on her laptop.

Chris kissed the top of her head. 'How long have you been up?'

'Since soon after you fell asleep,' she said. 'I was lying there thinking about all the work I needed to do, so I thought fuck it, I'll get up and do it.'

'Your mystery guest giving you a headache?'

She grimaced. 'Just a bit. On top of everything else.'

'Want to talk about it?' He knew she'd gone all sex kitten on him for a reason.

She sighed. 'It's just that when I said I'd take Max's job, I didn't realise how much paperwork I'd have to do.'

'Maybe I should've applied. Report-writing will be all I'm good for before long,' he said.

'Oh, I can think of one or two things you're still good for.' She winked.

Chris ignored the comment. 'Drink?'

'Okay.' Hannah sat back and regarded him. 'So come on then, Detective, what's your take on this Chloe business?'

'It can't be her, can it? I saw her body with my own eyes.'

'It's just that this woman, whoever she is, seems to know so much about past events. She refers to Jen as Lisa. And there was a comment she made about how well James had aged. Who but Chloe would know all this stuff?'

'But we both know it can't be her.' Chris filled the kettle. 'DNA doesn't lie, does it, so how can it be her?'

'Poor Jen's out of her mind with worry, wondering if her family is safe.'

'Didn't you say they'd sent the kids to their grandparents?' Chris asked.

Hannah frowned. 'Yeah, but what if Jen's whole family is in danger?'

'I'm sure James can handle himself,' Chris said. 'I've seen evidence of that first hand.'

'Then, on top of all of this going on, I've just been told that a wanted criminal is back in the UK.' She leaned back in her chair and closed her eyes.

'What? You're stressing because you've got more than one case to handle? Welcome to my world.' Chris poured hot water into mugs.

'I know I've had it easy so far, but still . . .'

'So, what are you going to do, Detective?'

Opening her eyelids, Hannah sat erect and focused on Chris. 'I've asked Jen to take over the Chloe case for me.'

This came as a surprise. He'd assumed Hannah would want that for herself. 'Wow. And her reaction?'

'There was a definite gleam in her eyes when I told her. She wants in again.'

'Problem solved then,' he said.

Hannah sipped at her drink several times, clearly building up courage for something. Then she said, 'Would you go to Reading with her in the morning and talk to Adam Coulthard?'

'Me?'

'Yeah, you. I hear you were a pretty fine officer at one time, Detective Inspector Jackson.'

'Ha, now I know you're lying. I'm signed off, remember, as in unfit for purpose.'

'I could really do with your help on this case, Chris,' she said.

He slumped into a chair opposite her. 'I don't know. I'm a bit of a liability at the moment.'

'Ah, but you're my liability, Detective.'

* * *

Chris couldn't believe what he was about to agree to. Was he ready to go back out into the field? He wasn't exactly match-fit, needing as he did those regular afternoon naps. Plus, he hadn't cleared the air with Jen after what had happened in the lift that time.

'Hannah, what if I fall apart again?' he whispered.

She put her arms around him. 'Then I'll pick you up again.'

'Guess I'd better get some sleep then, if I've got work to do tomorrow.'

'Want me to come and tuck you in?' she purred.

'You've got reports to write, remember.'

'How could I forget?'

How he'd hated Hannah's world. Everything decided on the spur of the moment. The recklessness with which she plunged into action. And here he was, agreeing to go back. Why?

CHAPTER 38

November 2021

With the return of speech, a memory surfaces. This morning I awoke with a name on my lips. Maria. Who is she, and why does her name seem so significant?

* * *

'Good morning, beautiful,' Sean says. He is always there, attentive, concerned, but I have no memory of him.

'Hey.' Still drowsy, my reply is thick, slurred.

'How are you feeling this morning?' The nurse is always here too, and she always goes through the same routine. 'Can you move your legs for me? Great. We'll soon have you walking again.'

If only. I long to feel the sun on my face. Meanwhile, I'm still flat on my back, hooked up to all these machines . . . beep beep beep.

'Your reflexes are good this morning,' the nurse says. 'I'll speak to the consultant about getting you detached from some of these machines.' I smile, and Sean squeezes my hand.

I'm beginning to remember the car crash, but everything else is a blank. Sean says he's been told not to tell me anything, that I need to *remember stuff for myself — something about planting "false memories". As the nurse drones on, my mind is on that name, Maria, and why she seems so important to me. I'll ask Sean later. Surely for once he'll break his vow of silence.*

Finally, the nurse exits the room, leaving Sean and I alone. Usually he just sits and watches me, but today he is excited at the prospect of taking me home for a visit. He tells me he's cleaned the house up, and that all my friends are looking forward to seeing me after all this time. It's just a shame I can't remember who they are.

Okay, here we go. 'Sean, please tell me — who is Maria?'

He looks blank. 'Who?'

'Maria. The name has just come to me, and I feel like I should know her.'

'Sorry, love, but I have no idea. I have never heard of a Maria.'

'Maybe she's someone in my family.' As I speak, it hits me. Sean is my only visitor. Why haven't any of my relatives come to see me?

'Sean, where's my family?'

'To be honest with you, Chloe, I don't know. Ever since we've been together it's just been me and you.'

I search my memory for some indication, some faint impression. Surely I'd remember my mother. But except for this one name, it's a blank.

Tears roll on to my cheeks. 'Am I going to be like this for ever?'

Sean comes and sits on the bed. 'It'll take time. You've had a serious head injury.'

'Yeah yeah, post-traumatic amnesia.' I parrot the doctors' words.

'It will come, don't worry,' Sean says.

'I just wish I knew who she was.'

CHAPTER 39

Jen Garner
2023

Jen found Chris waiting outside Hannah's apartment. She leaned over from the driver's seat and opened the passenger door for him, averting her eyes while he hauled himself and his stick into the car. She pulled away and they drove in a silence that grew more awkward with every mile.

Chris cleared his throat. 'Does he know we're coming?'

'Yeah. We're going to see him at his work. It sounds like he's turned his life around — he's a sales manager at a car-manufacturing company on the outskirts of Reading. Greenwing Automotive.'

'Ah. I've never actually met him.'

'Really? Oh yeah, I'd forgotten. It was just Hannah and me. He had some pretty heavy gang affiliations back then.'

'Hannah told me you had him down as Chloe's killer,' Chris said.

She grimaced. 'I was hell-bent on avenging my best friend's death at one point.'

They fell silent again.

'Jen, about what happened on the last case,' Chris began. 'I was in denial, you know, about my illness, and trying to prove that I could still do the things I used to do.'

'You were being reckless,' she said.

'I was. I should never have dragged you along with me. That was unforgivable.'

'You know, if you'd have just spoken to me, Chris, I'd have supported you. Instead—'

'Then word got round that I'd fallen,' he continued, 'and when I buckled in front of you all, well, I just lost my head.'

'We'd have got there in the end,' she said.

'I know I stepped out of line. I just had this idea that me and the famous Lisa Carter were invincible.'

'I'd stopped being Lisa Carter long before then.'

'I know, and I'm sorry.'

Jen laughed. 'Just count yourself lucky I never told James.'

Chris grinned. 'Still my biggest fan, is he?'

'He's warming to you,' Jen said. 'I'm always here if you need someone to talk to, you know. I would have been back then too.'

'I might take you up on that.' He flicked at his leg. 'I'm still trying to find my way around this disease.'

'And I promise I won't go telling tales to Hannah,' she added.

'Thank you, Jen.'

They fell into a more comfortable silence. Jen wondered how it was going to feel talking to Adam again, having had no contact with him since the trial. How was he going to react when he discovered that Chloe could quite possibly still be alive?

'Chris, do you think we should tell Adam about that woman claiming to be Chloe?'

'I don't know,' he said. 'I haven't really thought about it, to be honest. Basically, I'm along for the ride.'

'Hannah ask you to keep an eye on me, did she?'

He shrugged. 'I think she's in a panic, suddenly having these two cases landed on her.'

CHAPTER 40

DI Chris Jackson

'Thank you for agreeing to see us,' Jen said. She held out her hand, but instead of shaking it, Adam gave her a hug.

'Good to see you again, Jen.'

'DI Chris Jackson.' Chris held out his hand, hoping he wasn't going to get one too.

'Glad you told me you were coming this time, instead of kicking my door in.' Adam laughed. 'My office is this way.'

Adam led them along a maze of corridors amid the sound of automatic drills and the smell of lacquer. 'Are you a car person, Detective?' he asked.

'I am, but unfortunately my pay packet doesn't stretch to fast cars,' Chris replied.

'Well, if you're interested, I'll take you on a tour when we're finished.'

'That would be good, thank you.'

Adam showed them into a plush office at least twice the size of Chris's — that was if he still had an office.

'If it hadn't been for Chloe dying, none of this would have been possible,' Adam said. Jen shot Chris a look. 'What I meant was that the shock of her death gave me the push I needed to straighten up my life and finally get out of the drugs world.'

'Ah, I see. Well, I'm glad to hear some good came of it,' Jen said. 'I guess your previous experience in, er, sales helped you land this gig.'

He grinned. 'At least I don't have to resort to violence to get my commission.'

'Now, down to the reason we're here,' Jen began. 'Has anyone been in contact with you about Chloe?'

'No. No one knew we were together, other than you and that woman you were with last time,' he said.

'Hannah. Well, there's been some strange rumours doing the rounds about Chloe.'

Adam frowned. 'Strange how?'

Jen paused, clearly wondering how to word the bombshell. 'Believe it or not, word has it that she is still alive.'

'Well, that's nothing but a load of rubbish, isn't it? You mean you came all the way here to ask me about some story?'

'Well, yes,' Jen said. 'We had to be sure, because if she is still alive, you'd be the first person she'd have contacted.'

'You've both had a wasted journey then. No one has contacted me. Hang on, you don't mean to say that someone is pretending to be my dead girlfriend?'

'That's why Jen and I wanted to speak to you directly,' Chris said.

'There's some sick people out there.' Adam shook his head, disgusted. 'Well, you can be sure that if anyone comes to me with that kind of bullshit, I'll be demanding answers from them.'

'Let's hope we can put a stop to it before it goes too far,' Jen added.

'I'm glad you told me, though. I'll keep my ears to the ground.'

'Thank you, Adam,' she said.

Adam stood up. 'So, how about that tour then, Detectives?'

CHAPTER 41

Adam Coulthard
November 2021

There was nothing I could do but return to my life in Reading. Believing I'd found her again brought back all the pain of her loss, throwing me into an endless cycle of drugs and television — anything to forget. But I couldn't get that woman's face out of my mind. She'd looked so scared, and I hadn't meant to frighten her. Days went by like this, until I decided to return to Chessington and apologise to her. I'd explain that she looked exactly like the love of my life, who was dead.

I booked the same room in the same hotel and began my search again. Now I knew where she lived, I believed it would be easy to find her. I'd twice seen her in the marketplace; all I had to do was wait. I spent the days at Chessington market and my nights at the flats where she lived. But she was nowhere to be seen.

I went into a newsagent looking for something to read to pass the time, where I spotted a local newspaper with the headline *Unknown woman found in wreckage following car crash.* Something made me buy a copy of the paper — or was I just clutching at straws?

An unnamed woman drove her car into the barrier on the M1 in the early hours of yesterday morning. Police reports say she was speeding at over 100 miles per hour. The black Ford Fiesta . . . Hang on, hadn't that woman run towards a black Fiesta? No, it had to be a coincidence. I read on:

The woman, who has yet to be identified, was extracted from the car by the fire service and rushed to Chessington Hospital, where she remains in a critical condition.

Back at the hotel, I searched my phone for news reports of the accident. If this was the same woman, maybe there was a way I could get Chloe back.

CHAPTER 42

November 2021

I thought I was imagining it at first, but I keep seeing the same person walking past my room and peering in at me. He's not one of the medical staff. He always stops at the door to my room, like he's trying to decide whether or not to come in. He never comes when Sean is here, only when I'm alone. After it's been going on for a while, I ask the nurse about him.

'Who's that man I see walking past my room?'

'Which man is that, sweetie?'

'He comes past every day, usually just before lunch. He stops at the door and hovers there, sort of hesitating.'

'It must be one of the doctors, dear.'

'No, it's definitely not a doctor. I've lain here long enough to know all the staff. He doesn't wear a hospital uniform or a white coat.'

'Then I don't know, but I can assure you that we don't allow people to wander into the ward without a reason for being here.'

'Then who is he?' My patience is running out. The nurse doesn't seem to know who I mean, and Sean's never mentioned seeing him either. I can't shake the feeling that I'm being watched and I don't know why or by whom. I'm still practically bed-bound and need help to get around. Next time he passes, I'm going to shout at him. Then they'll know.

CHAPTER 43

Hannah Littlefair
2023

Hannah strode into the office. 'Have we got a visual on Kristoff?'

'No, boss, not since the airport.'

'How the hell did you lose him?' No one answered. 'Selina, Georgina, can I see you in my office, please?' The two young women exchanged anxious glances. 'Don't look so worried. You haven't done anything wrong. Look, I know you are busy with other stuff, but whatever you're working on at the moment, I need you to stop and concentrate on our imposter.'

More anxious looks. 'Okaaay.'

'I know you've both been working on different aspects of the case, so I thought you'd be best suited to the job.'

'Sounds good to me,' Selina said.

'Jen and Chris Jackson are on their way back from Reading now. They've been speaking to the man Chloe was engaged to prior to her death. You will be reporting to Jen.'

'Lisa Carter? Awesome!' Selina looked delighted.

'Yes, I'm sure you've heard all about her. She is one of the greatest officers of our time, so you can learn a lot from her.'

'And Chris Jackson? Where does he come into it?' Georgina asked.

'He's the DI of one of Nottingham's Special Ops units. Chris was the SIO on the original investigation into Chloe's death, so, as you can imagine, he has an interest in her supposed return to life.'

'Great.'

'You'll be based in the meeting room, along with Chris and Jen.'

Georgina nodded. 'Is there anything we can do regarding the Kristoff situation while we wait for them to return?'

'No, you can start by getting everything set up so you can begin as soon as they get back.'

After they'd hurried out, chattering excitedly, Hannah decided to read over Elispeth's report from the previous day. She had to keep reminding herself that the woman in the safe house wasn't Chloe. Some of the things Elispeth had reported made her wonder. The imposter had spoken of matters only Chloe would know about. Doubts began creeping into Hannah's mind.

While she pondered the problem, Jen and Chris returned. Hannah noticed that Chris was back to using his stick. Not a good sign. 'Come through to the office,' she said. 'It'll be a bit more comfortable in there.'

Jen made herself at home on the sofa, leaning back and tucking her feet beneath her. Chris, however, remained standing rather awkwardly, his back against the wall.

'Before we start, I've managed to get you a small team to assist you,' Hannah told them.

Jen looked relieved. 'Okay.' She changed her position on the sofa and looked over towards Chris.

'Does that mean you won't be needing me then?' He sounded hopeful.

'No such luck, Detective Jackson. Your input could be vital.'

He said nothing. Hannah was subjected to yet more indecision. Had she been wrong in assuming that he wanted back in?

* * *

After her meeting with Chris and Jen, Hannah went in search of Tim. 'Have Nottingham sent the case files yet?'

'I'm just about to chase them up,' he said.

'When they arrive, would you make copies for me, please? Discreetly.'

'Of course.' Tim gave her a knowing look.

She hated the thought of him having something on her, but she needed to ease her mind.

CHAPTER 44

Jen Garner

Jen had watched Hannah and Tim with interest. Something was going on there.

She joined the others in the meeting room, where Hannah was holding a briefing. 'I'm a woman of many talents—' there were laughs from around the room — 'but we have two major cases on our hands right now, and I can't be in two places at the same time. I have therefore decided to hand over the Chloe investigation to Jen — or, as you should refer to her from now on, Lisa. We can't afford for the imposter to learn her real identity.'

'It's my case starting from now?' Jen asked.

'Yep,' Hannah said. 'The room is yours.'

Shit. She'd been hoping for a bit of time to prepare. She looked at Chris, who was staring into space, as if he were wishing himself elsewhere. The others were waiting expectantly.

'Erm, okay, well, I'm Jen Garner. You may know me by my cover name of Lisa Carter — or will from now on, at least. You'll be glad to know that I'm somewhat older and wiser now . . .' More laughs from the team. 'Basically, this case involves a woman who has turned up insisting that she's Chloe Seaward. Since Chloe was murdered two years ago, this woman has to be an imposter. What we need to find out now is who she is, who sent her and with what aim.'

'I led the team that carried out the investigation into the real Chloe's death.' Chris suddenly emerged from his trance. 'And I am absolutely certain that the body we identified was Chloe. A leading pathologist examined the body and performed an autopsy. What is more, the results from the DNA test confirmed that the body was indeed Chloe Seaward.'

'Thank you, Chris. Apologies, I didn't introduce you properly. This is DI Chris Jackson. He heads the Nottingham Special Ops team to which I belong.' For the moment Jen had forgotten that she'd been all but fired. 'After I left the Met, no one knew my address or my new identity. Yet, two nights ago, this woman turned up on my doorstep calling me Lisa — a name I ceased to use when I left the service.

'Today, Chris and I visited Adam Coulthard, who was Chloe's fiancé at the time of her death. He told us that he hasn't seen Chloe nor has anyone approached him regarding her. At the time of her death, he was connected to a number of gangs, but since then he appears to have turned his life around, and now has a good job and a steady income. He says that Chloe helped him to go straight.'

'I'm guessing we looked into him at the time of Chloe's murder?' Georgina said.

'Briefly. But we lost interest in him after the investigating team concluded that he wasn't responsible for Chloe's death,' Jen replied.

'Something that doesn't quite add up in my mind is the fact that he's gone from drug dealer to sales manager of a car company in just two years,' Chris said.

Jen nodded. 'I've been thinking the same thing, Chris.'

'Shall I look into him then?' Georgina asked.

'Please — although weren't you looking into how our imposter got to my house?'

110

'Oh yes. Sorry. Do you want me to stick with that?'

Jen looked to Hannah, not knowing these detectives or their capabilities.

'Selina, would you be happy to look into Adam Coulthard?' Hannah said.

'Can do.'

Georgina looked deep in thought. 'Could Adam be using the cars from his company to smuggle drugs?'

Jen nodded again. 'Good point.'

'Georgina, do you want to fill us in on how our imposter got to Lisa's?' Hannah said.

CHAPTER 45

DI Chris Jackson

Slumped in his chair, Chris wondered what exactly he was doing here. Sure, like everyone he was curious to know who this woman was. More importantly, he needed to know if his team had messed up in their investigation into Chloe's death. But having to listen to *the* Lisa Carter in full flow wasn't his idea of fun. All the others — including Hannah — were obviously in awe of her. Maybe he was missing something. The truth was, he was weary. After a relatively sleepless night, he'd been dragged off to Reading and back and he was having trouble staying awake. He couldn't expect much rest at Hannah's either, given that whenever she was under stress she'd go into sex kitten mode to ease the tension. Well, his body just couldn't handle it anymore.

The sound of his name broke through his thoughts. 'Chris? Nottingham is your patch,' Jen was saying.

'Sorry?'

'Georgina was just telling us that our imposter arrived into Long Eaton via a train from Nottingham.'

'I've not really had a chance to look into it yet,' Georgina said.

Chris sighed inwardly. Now he'd be in trouble with Hannah for not listening. 'Well,' he said, 'I guess the first place to look would be the CCTV cameras.'

'Do you think you could work with Georgina on that?' Jen asked him.

'Sure.' In Nottingham, he was Jen's boss, but now he was being asked to work under her. Chris wasn't sure how he felt about that.

'Elliot, I understand from Hannah that you are monitoring what goes on inside the house, is that right?'

'Yes, ma'am, we have recording devices in place there.'

'Please, it's J— Lisa.' She smiled at the young, nervous detective.

'I'm rotating with Ashley so that both of us stay fresh and alert, m— er, Lisa.'

'Good idea,' she said.

Hannah glanced at her watch. 'Shall we move on to Elispeth's report?'

'Of course.'

'Some of the stuff she's telling Elispeth concerns previous cases that only Chloe should have known about,' Hannah said.

By now, Chris was really struggling to stay awake. Jen glanced at him and said, 'Well, I guess we'd all better get on then. Unless anyone has any questions?' No one spoke.

As the others were gathering their stuff and preparing to leave the room, Chris caught Hannah's attention. 'Can I have a word?'

'Yeah, of course. Come through to my office,' she said.

'Are you free to help me when you've spoken to Hannah?' Georgina asked.

Chris's heart sank. 'Give me five and I'll be with you.' So much for his nap.

113

CHAPTER 46

Hannah Littlefair

Hannah closed the door to her office and turned to Chris. 'Everything okay?'

'Han, I don't see why I need to be here,' he said.

'What do you mean? I thought you'd be itching to find out who our mystery person is.'

'But I'm not going to be much use.'

'Well, I *am* surprised. I expected more from you,' she said.

'Hannah, I'm tired. My body is falling apart, I've been to Reading and back today after barely sleeping last night, I just can't do it.' Chris sighed. 'Look, I love you with all my heart, but I can't cope with your sex kitten act every time you get stressed.'

She frowned. 'I didn't hear you complaining last night.'

'It was great when I was in Derby and you were here,' he continued. 'I'd see you occasionally and we'd have great sex. But every night . . . it's too much for me.'

'You want me to ease off?' She felt hurt.

'I don't know. I'm just trying to do what's best for me and this faulty body of mine.'

114

'It'll be a pity. Georgina seems pretty keen to work with *the* DI Chris Jackson,' Hannah said.

'Does she really need my help? After all, I'm just a street-level police officer. I bet she's more highly qualified than I am.'

'Yes, but she doesn't have your street savvy, and she doesn't know Nottingham like you do.'

He sighed. 'I just can't see any point in me staying. My input will be minimal, and on top of that, I can't handle you.'

'Now you're being silly.'

'Am I?'

'I want you to stay, Chris. You must have questions about this woman. Don't you want to know who she is?'

It was his turn to furrow his brow. 'I was quite happy with the work I did on that case.'

'So? No one's accusing you of anything,' she said. 'Stay and see this one through. Look, I'll put you up in a hotel so you're away from me and my wayward demands. How's that?'

'Hannah, do you remember the reason you bought me that donkey?'

'The sponsorship thing? Yeah, when we saw the advert on TV it reminded me of you.'

'Because they can work for hours on end, often carrying back-breaking loads,' he said.

'Like you, and the way you always took on too much . . .' Hannah stopped, realising what Chris was trying to say.

'I want to be with you, Hannah. I'm just worried that I won't be able to cope.'

'Why don't we just agree that you can come and go as you please. You can choose the hours you work, and I'll be on my best behaviour at bedtimes.'

'I'm sorry, Hannah,' Chris said. 'I know how stupid it sounds—'

'Chris, I love you, and if I need to change in order to be with you, I will.'

'Thank you.' He kissed her.

They were interrupted by a tap at the door. 'Excuse me, Hannah.'

'Oh, Tim, what can I do for you?'

'I just wanted to bring you the files. They've also been sent to your email.' Tim handed her a Manila folder.

'Thank you, Tim.' He exited, closing the door behind him.

'Anything interesting?' Chris asked.

'It's to do with the Kristoff case.' She shoved the folder in her drawer. If Chris discovered that she was checking on the work he'd done, it would need more than a kiss to make it better.

CHAPTER 47

DI Chris Jackson

'DI Jackson.' Georgina slid back her chair.

'Please, it's Chris,' he said. 'I'm not sure how much use I'll be. I'm completely shattered, to be honest.'

She smiled. 'You'll get used to it.'

If only, he thought. Chris wondered if it was the extra drugs he was taking that was making him so tired. Getting used to the work was one thing, but when was he going to get used to having MS? 'So. What do you need from me, Georgina?'

'Hannah said you'd be able to help me with tracing this woman's movements, since you know the place better than me.'

'I think she was trying to give me a job I could do.' Chris pulled up a chair and sat down. 'Right. What have we got?'

'Well, I've got her getting off the train in Long Eaton.' Georgina selected the clip from the CCTV recording.

Chris watched a woman closely resembling Chloe walk along the platform. 'Good job the station was pretty quiet.'

'Now here we have the feed from the cameras at Nottingham train station, where the train originated.'

'Hang on, is this live now?' Chris watched various trains pull in and out of the station.

'Yes,' Georgina said. 'We have access to every camera in the UK.'

It suddenly occurred to Chris that when he wanted to view the footage of Nottingham that disappeared, the Met could have removed the footage that had been lost, making it harder for him to track Jen through Nottingham. 'So if, say, one of your detectives appeared in the recording doing something illegal, could you erase the footage?'

Georgina looked perplexed. 'Not me, no, but Hannah would be able to.'

Chris frowned. *Interesting.*

'Anyway,' she continued.

He jumped. 'Sorry, I was away with the fairies.'

'Thinking about the footage of your drunken nights out?' Georgina laughed. 'Where I'm stuck is trying to find where our mystery guest could have come from. I can't find a single shot of her on any of the cameras before the feed we just saw of her getting off. Mercifully there was only one stop between Nottingham and Long Eaton on this journey — Beeston — so there aren't many stations to check, but it's like a—'

'Needle in a haystack?'

Georgina laughed. 'In a mountain.'

'Okay, can you get up a map of Nottingham? Let's start there,' Chris said.

'Here we are.'

'Get it printed off and we'll begin our search. Give me a nudge if I fall asleep, won't you?'

'I might just tell the boss you're asleep on the job and get you sacked.'

Chris laughed. 'If only.'

CHAPTER 48

Jen Garner

'Those two seem to be working well together,' Jen said to Hannah. 'I think I even heard Chris laughing at one point.'

Hannah looked up from her desk. 'Good. I'm glad he's distracted.'

'Why? What's up?' Jen asked.

'Jen, I need you to seriously keep this between the two of us.'

Jen sat down. 'Oh God, what's he done now?'

'I'm worried about the original Chloe investigation,' Hannah said.

'How do you mean?'

'To what extent did Chris's team actually carry him on that case? I didn't know he was having problems and I'm his girlfriend.'

'But you said yourself, Hannah, you chose to ignore the signs that something was wrong,' Jen said.

'Forget about me. How long had Chris been hiding what was going on with him from his team?'

Jen furrowed her brow. 'I don't quite get where this is going.'

'Suppose that *is* Chloe Seaward, and the investigation into the dead woman was a cock-up?'

'Do you really think Max wouldn't have gone through her case files? The bloke never used to sleep.'

'You've seen how Chris is now, Jen. He isn't his usual self. It's like this diagnosis has taken part of him away.'

'The DI Jackson we know thrived when he was knee-deep in a case—'

Hannah's interruption was frantic. 'Are you saying he needs to go back to Nottingham and work?'

'I'm saying he needs something to get his teeth into,' Jen said.

'You'll laugh at this, Jen. He told me he can't handle the sexual side of our relationship. He says I'm too much for him. I mean, what the fuck?'

'Maybe he's right. He's ill, Hannah.'

'Yeah, he said that.'

'You're amazing, Hannah, you really are. Just let him be, and don't let your need for sex kill what you have with him.'

'But what about me?' Hannah almost wailed.

'There are other ways that don't involve male participation, you know.' Jen felt like they were back at school, gossiping about who'd done what and with whom. 'Keep hold of what you've got with Chris and, for God's sake, don't let him go. He's a good guy and there's not many of them around.'

'Thanks, Jen.'

'Any time. And just make sure you tell that devil on your shoulder that Max would have checked the Chloe case files. If there was anything amiss, he'd have been on it.'

CHAPTER 49

Hannah Littlefair

Hannah knew Jen was right about Chris, but she had never been with a man who had told her he couldn't cope with her sexual demands. Maybe she just needed to let Chris be her calming influence. Why could she never give herself wholeheartedly to someone? Was she afraid of getting hurt? After he'd ended it so abruptly that time, she had cursed herself for letting her guard down. Yet she had been so relieved when she found out why he had ended it like he had. Now she was doubting his work, all of it, even from before they met.

* * *

Hannah wandered into the meeting room, where they were all busily working away. 'Selina, did you find anything out about Adam?'

'No, boss. Just that he seems to have been on the straight and narrow since we sent the Crawfords down.'

'How did he get the job with the car manufacturers?' Jen asked.

Selina shrugged. 'Like everyone does, I guess. He went for an interview.'

'I suppose his years selling drugs for the Crawfords gave him plenty of experience in sales,' Hannah said.

Chris ignored her joke. 'What I don't understand is how he got himself appointed a manager.'

'Is it worth contacting their HR department?' Selina suggested.

'We need to be careful, because if he didn't disclose his past — remember, he's never been convicted — we could lose him his job,' Hannah warned.

Jen laughed. 'I don't want him hating me all over again.' She was well aware that he held her partly responsible for Chloe's death.

'We needn't ask them in person. After all, they'll have his file on the computer. We just need to get into their system. I'll issue you with a code when we're done here.' Hannah still wasn't used to having to issue codes to her officers. It felt to her like the Met were tightening their grip, and wanted to control every single thing its officers did.

'Can I suggest that we also look at who else works for the company? You know, maybe he got the job through a mate,' Chris said.

'I'm not one hundred per cent clear why we're looking into Adam in the first place,' Selina said, 'other than the fact that he was Chloe's fiancé.'

'It may not even be connected with our imposter,' Hannah said. 'It was just that Chris and Lisa were surprised at his sudden rise to manager, which I agree is a tad suspicious. Plus, if Chloe is alive, why hasn't she been in touch with him? It's one of the main reasons why I'm certain that woman isn't who she says she is.'

By now, Chris really did seem to be on the verge of nodding off. She needed to either send him home or book him into a hotel. 'Go home,' she whispered in his ear. 'Or to a hotel, if you'd rather. Either way, go somewhere and get some sleep.'

'You sure?' Chris questioned.

'Of course. Anyway, I need you to keep the bed warm for me.'

'Right, well, that's me off then.' Chris got to his feet. 'Since the boss has told me to go home, who am I to argue?'

'If there isn't a car waiting downstairs, call me on my mobile and I'll sort one,' Hannah said.

'Don't get lost,' Georgina chimed in.

'Ha, I think my bed is calling me, so I'll just follow the sound of it if I get lost. Until tomorrow, comrades.'

Hopefully, that meant he'd be back tomorrow. She'd give him a couple of hours and then drop him a message. At the very least she ought to know where he was.

'So—' Chris now absent, Hannah turned back to face Jen — 'Detective Garner, what are your thoughts?'

'Georgina,' Jen said, 'where are you with tracing our imposter's route to mine?'

'We knew she had to have got on at either Nottingham or Beeston, but we found more footage from inside the carriage that indicates it was the former. Chris — I mean DI Jackson — gave me some great pointers about how she might have got to the train station there, but I still can't find where she actually got on the train.'

'How does that make sense? You're certain she got on at Nottingham, yet you don't know where? You're telling me she just materialises out of nowhere?' Jen's voice was laced with frustration.

'Yes, well . . .' Georgina composed herself under Jen's scrutiny. 'The footage shows her looking for her seat and sitting down before the train arrives at Beeston, but as for before then . . . the platforms at Nottingham were packed solid at the time. The carriages filled up almost instantly, standing room and all.'

Jen's eyes narrowed. 'Basically, she was hiding in plain sight.'

'I hate to say this, but she has done exactly as we're trained to do and avoid detection, as protocol dictates,' Georgina said.

'Fine, but then she breaks protocol by turning up at Lisa's,' Hannah countered.

Jen paused for a moment, clearly deep in thought. 'Georgina, have you checked the cameras on the train from before she takes her seat? I'm wondering if maybe she got on somewhere and hid in the toilets until the train reached Nottingham.'

Georgina looked confused. 'But the train originated in Nottingham. How could she have got on anywhere else?'

'Think about it. The train may have originated there, but it had to have terminated there first from a previous journey before departing again. She could have got on earlier in the day at a stop further down the line, waited out of sight, then emerged once the train was ready to leave Nottingham again,' Jen explained.

'Oh, that's a good point,' Georgina said. 'I'll look into that now.'

'Elliot, how're things in the safe house?' Hannah asked.

'Pretty quiet. Dr Spellbound cut the feed while he spoke to her,' Elliot said.

Hannah smiled. 'Quiet couple of hours for you, then.'

'Indeed. Though before they cut it, I picked up Elispeth trying to bond with the imposter.'

'Good. Elispeth is doing just as I asked.'

'Fingers crossed it works then,' Jen said. 'Where are we with the DNA?'

'Well, they took a sample yesterday, and we put a rush on it, so hopefully late today or, knowing our luck, tomorrow,' Hannah replied.

'Well, let's hope the results prove once and for all who she really is,' Jen sighed. 'I'm getting sick of waiting.'

CHAPTER 50

November 2021

'Oh my God, Sean, I'm so glad you're here.'

Sean hurries over to my bed and takes hold of my hand. 'What's the matter?'

'That man. I know who he is.' By now I've been sweating so much the sheets are clinging to my body.

'What man?' Sean sits down on the bed.

'The man that's been walking up and down the ward looking into my room.'

'You haven't told me about this.' It's true. I'd forgotten that I hadn't told him.

'Sorry, it was the nurse I told. You see, there's this man that comes into the ward every day and just walks up and down, looking into my room. I've just remembered who he is.' My mind is the clearest it's been since I regained consciousness.

Sean looks at me, concerned. 'Hush now, Chloe, it's okay.'

'But it's not, Sean. I think I'm in danger.'

'You're perfectly safe here.'

'Sean, he's a drug dealer. He's trying to kidnap me.'

Sean stares at me. 'Drug dealer? What are you talking about?'

'I was on a train and he was sitting opposite me with this gun pointed at me under the table. I was trying to signal to the people passing by, but no one even looked at me.'

Just then, my nurse enters the room. 'Tell him!' I cry. 'Tell him what I told you.' But the nurse just looks at me blankly. 'The man! The man that keeps checking on me. I know who he is. He's trying to kidnap me.'

'I don't think he is, Chloe,' she says.

'He tried before. I was on a train and he had a gun pointing at me!' Concerned, the nurse checks the monitor. The needle shows my heart racing far too fast.

'Chloe, you need to calm down, sweetie.'

'Why doesn't anyone believe me? He's come back for me, I'm telling you.' The nurse and Sean exchange looks. I refuse to just lie there and wait for him to come for me. I throw off the sheets and swing my legs over the side of the bed.

The nurse is now annoyed. 'Chloe! Stay in your bed. You know you're not strong enough to walk yet.'

I sway on my feet. Sean catches hold of me and lowers me back on to the bed.

By now I'm crying. 'I'm telling you, someone is trying to kill me. No one believes me.'

'I believe you,' Sean says. He swings my legs back and replaces the sheet. 'Calm down, Chloe. Come on, you're safe here. The nurse is here with you.'

'And you're not leaving here unless I say so.' The woman wears a reassuring smile.

'But what if he tries to take me when you're not here? You can't always be here.'

'I'll tell the other staff to keep an eye out, okay?' the nurse replies.

'And I can stay here longer if you want,' Sean says.

'What about your job?'

'Chloe, you're the most important thing in the world to me, okay? More important than work.'

But I know I'm not safe. I need to get out of here somehow.

'When can I go home?' I ask. He won't find me there.

'Soon,' the nurse says. 'When the cut on your head is healing nicely, and we're sure your recovery is going well.'

'I can't bear being stuck in here. I want to go home,' I shout.

'How about I go and get us a cup of coffee?' Sean suggests. I know what he wants. He wants to speak to the nurse about me.

The nurse beams. 'Yes, what a good idea.' Then she heads towards her office from where she can watch me. Maybe she's in on this. Maybe I'm being kept here under false pretences.

When she's gone, Sean comes back and whispers in my ear. 'You're starting to remember, but we can't talk about it here. Just hang on and concentrate on your recovery.' I stare at him, my mind full of a thousand questions. 'Just act normal, okay, and we'll have you out of here in no time.' Then he gets up and leaves the room, while I lie back and try to work out what he meant.

* * *

Sean Sterling

Sean was heading off to get himself something to drink when the nurse called him over.

'I know it's hard, but you handled that very well. Don't worry about what she says; it's just the brain trying to heal itself. While she's going through this process her dreams will feel very real to her.'

'I . . . she just looked so scared, like it really had happened.'

'If it puts your mind at ease, she was peacefully asleep before you arrived.'

CHAPTER 51

Jen Garner
2023

She was exactly where she wanted to be — in charge of this case. So why couldn't she shake the feeling that she shouldn't be here? She had felt very differently when she was working with Chris and his team. Back then, all she'd wanted to do was go and kick down some doors and make the others see where they were going wrong. Now she had the power, there were no doors to kick, no one to arrest. She was in limbo. Reason told her there was no way Chloe Seaward could be sitting in that safe house. Her heart told her otherwise. That it was her best friend sitting in that cottage being subjected to lie detector tests when she should be welcomed back with open arms. Then there was James and the kids. James wanted her back home, not here, miles from him and the family. What was it about this place that kept dragging her back, no matter how hard she tried to let go? She hadn't mentioned it to Hannah, who was under enough stress as it was, but if that woman *was* Chloe, the entire case against Jessica would be at stake. Jessica had pleaded not guilty to killing Chloe, so if Chloe was alive, Jessica was indeed innocent. Everything felt so goddamn messed up and there was no one she could talk to about it. Not James, that was for sure; he just wouldn't understand. Life had been so easy when she was Lisa Carter. Everything made sense and she didn't have to face the consequences.

'Lisa. Lisa?' Selina was standing in front of her.

'Sorry, I was miles away. What's up?'

'Hannah's just been told that Dr Spellbound is on his way back with his findings. The call came while you were daydreaming.'

'Thanks, hun. That obvious, huh?'

Selina laughed. 'Let's just say that I've been trying to get your attention for at least five minutes.'

'How have you got on with accessing Adam's HR file?'

'Yeah, about that,' she said. 'I don't seem to be getting anywhere, and I could really use your expertise.'

'Now that might be a bit of a challenge, seeing how rusty I am. Let me see the doctor and then I'll be over. All right?'

'Thanks, I'd appreciate that.'

Jen shook herself. She really needed to get her shit together because this meeting with the doc could be the turning point in the case. They were still awaiting the DNA results, but if she had failed the lie detector test, they could at least start treating her as an imposter.

CHAPTER 52

Hannah Littlefair

Georgina showed Dr Spellbound into Hannah's office.

Hannah introduced herself. 'We spoke briefly on the phone. I'm sorry I haven't been able to speak to you before now. You wouldn't believe how busy I am.'

'Not a problem,' he said. 'Though I must say I don't think I've ever been called on to advise on quite so complex a case as this one.'

'Someone will be bringing coffee, and my colleague should be along shortly. Have you had to travel far to get here?' Hannah asked.

'I'm from Kettering of all places. It's been some time since I've done any work for the Met.'

'I'll get one of my drivers to take you home. It can't be much fun making this journey every day.'

He chuckled. 'Oh, you needn't worry on that score, Ms Littlefair. I always make sure your people put me up in a fancy Mayfair hotel.'

Jen came in with coffee, and the discussion began.

'As I said, this is not your run-of-the-mill imposter scenario. The young lady in Houghton isn't pretending to be someone she's not — she is totally convinced that she is Chloe Seaward. She has revealed details of past cases that only Ms Seaward would know. She frequently mentioned a Lisa Carter, which I understand is — or was — your cover name?' He glanced at Jen.

'Yes, that's right,' she said.

'According to her, she and Lisa were best friends. She even went so far as to say she lost Lisa to love.'

Jen frowned. 'It's true we were best friends. Are you saying then that she's telling the truth?'

'She didn't once contradict herself,' he replied. 'And she became quite irritated by my questions, as would anyone who was telling the truth. An imposter, on the other hand, would have remained calm.'

'Could someone have coached her on what to say?' Hannah said.

'That's a possibility, but if that's the case, she is a very good actress. Oh, and I conducted a basic medical examination.'

'Any surprises there?' Jen asked.

'No. This young woman is perfectly fit, and her height and weight more or less correspond to that of Chloe Seaward.'

'At the time of her death, Chloe's height was . . . hang on a minute . . .' Hannah consulted the Long Eaton case file detailing Chloe's murder. 'Ah, 160 centimetres and she weighed fifty kilos.'

'You said "more or less".' It came out of Jen's mouth sounding more like a statement than her seeking clarification.

The doctor nodded. 'This woman is just under 160 centimetres.'

'That means it isn't her,' Jen said.

'I don't think the slight difference in height is significant enough to warrant that conclusion, Detective,' he countered.

Hannah glared at Jen, then asked, 'So, what about the lie detector test?'

'She was telling the truth. The readings remained constant throughout,' he said. 'When I asked her if she knew Jen Garner she answered no, but there was no indication that she was lying.'

131

'She only ever knew me as Lisa. I only became Jen much later,' Jen explained.

'I also asked her if she was in a relationship, which she denied,' Dr Spellbound continued.

'Did you mention Adam Coulthard by name?' Hannah asked.

'I did, and she said she didn't know him.'

Jen clapped her hands. 'Then we've got her.'

Dr Spellbound shook his head. 'Not necessarily. I understand that none of you knew about Adam until after Chloe died.'

'Chloe was aware of the rule about not dating someone you're investigating,' Hannah said. 'She'd have schooled herself in remaining absolutely calm under interrogation.'

The doctor looked triumphant. 'Exactly. Which is why the case is so complicated. The real Chloe was trained not to give herself away — including if she were subjected to a lie detector test.'

So we're right back to the beginning, Hannah thought. 'Given the question of her undercover training, what do you think, Doctor? Is she Chloe Seaward?'

'I would say yes, she is, or at least someone who believes they are Chloe Seaward.'

'So, we wait for the DNA results,' Jen said.

'And if that proves that she is Chloe, then what?' Hannah absently tapped the Long Eaton case file on the desk.

'If this young woman proves not to be Chloe, you need to be very careful on how you break the news to her,' Dr Spellbound said, getting to his feet. 'If you need me to speak to the young woman again, I'll be perfectly happy to do so. I shall be in London for a few more days.'

CHAPTER 53

Jen Garner

Jen was sitting in Hannah's office pondering the doctor's words when there was a knock on the door.

Seeing Jen, Georgina hesitated. 'I, er, was hoping to speak to Hannah.'

'She's just seeing the doctor out. Anything I can do to help?'

'I guess so.' Saying nothing more, Georgina stood looking vaguely around the office.

'You can wait if you like. I'm sure Hannah won't be long.'

'I, er . . .'

'Is it something to do with the Chloe Seaward case?'

'Yes. Erm . . .'

'We'd better wait for Hannah then. I'll let you know when she reappears,' Jen said.

'Thanks, Lisa.' Georgina turned and fled. *Odd*, thought Jen. *Maybe she's scared of me*, though she didn't think she was being that harsh. Certainly not as tough as Lisa Carter had been in her day.

* * *

'Sorry,' Hannah said. 'That man does like to talk. Is everything okay — other than the obvious?'

'Yeah, Georgina just came in looking for you. She was acting a bit, well, strange.'

'Don't worry, she's always like that. I wonder if she's picked anything up from the CCTV.'

Jen shrugged.

'What?'

'Oh, nothing, I was just thinking about Chloe and all that.'

'Listen, Jen. I may be the big boss now, but I'm still your friend, you know.'

'Thanks, Hannah. That's good to know.'

'Now, let's go and see what's kicking off with Georgina.'

* * *

Hannah, followed by Jen, swept into the meeting room. 'Georgina, what did you want to say? Found out who our imposter is, have you?'

'Not quite. In fact, I think we might have a slight problem . . .'

'Go on.'

'The, er, the DNA people have been on the phone,' Georgina began.

'And?'

'Well . . .'

'For God's sake, woman, spit it out.' By this stage, Jen could happily have throttled Georgina.

'They have completed the tests, but they said there's a problem.'

Jen gritted her teeth. 'What kind of problem?'

'Basically, they've done the tests but there's been a complication with matching up the DNA markers. They're asking if we can wait till tomorrow.'

'I can't believe this!' Jen almost shouted. 'They know whether it's Chloe or not. Why can't they just cut the red tape and get to the damn reveal?'

'I'm sorry, Lisa.' By now Georgina looked like she was close to tears.

'So our imposter gets a reprieve.' Jen glowered at Hannah.

'Don't look at me,' Hannah said as she headed towards her office. 'I'll phone them now and find out what's going on.'

Jen had had enough. 'This is stupid. I'm going out. You have my mobile number if you need me.' She turned on her heels and marched out of the room. Sod the DNA tests. She didn't need any laboratory to prove whether or not her best friend was alive. She'd damn well do it herself.

CHAPTER 54

November 2021

I can't believe my eyes. Sean has just come into my room pushing a wheelchair.

'Madam,' he says. 'Your chariot awaits.'

'Sean? What's going on?'

'The doctors have agreed that I can take you out into the big wide world for an hour.'

'Really?' I look to my nurse, who nods. I was beginning to think this day would never come and I'd be stuck in this room for ever. Forgetting that my legs are still weak, I throw off my sheets, ready to jump off the bed.

'Woah. Hang on a minute,' Sean says. 'We need to get you wrapped up first. It's cold out there, you know.' I don't even know where my clothes are; it's been so long since I wore anything but hospital pyjamas.

'Is it cold?' I have no idea what time of year it is.

'It's warm in the sun.'

'I got these washed for the occasion.' I see that the nurse is holding my faithful trackie bottoms. She and Sean help me into them. 'Right. Sean and I will support you as you stand. Take it slowly now.'

Once I'm settled in the chair, Sean wheels me out of the hospital entrance. The feel of the sun on my face makes me want to cry. We move through the car park and on into the grounds. Away from the comings and goings, I hear birds singing in the trees. My cheeks are wet with tears.

'What's the matter, sweetheart? Are you in pain?' Sean crouches down in front of me.

'No, no. It's just . . . I never thought I'd hear birdsong again.'

'Chloe, honey, you'll be walking before long.'

'If you hadn't have found me, I'd probably still be lying in that hospital bed trying to remember who I am.'

'I'd have found you. And now I have, I'm never leaving you again. Now, come on, let's find somewhere to sit in the sun. Ah. Over there looks good to me.' Sean wheels me towards a bench that looks like it's in the perfect position. 'Now, do you want me to lift you on to the bench, or are you okay to stay in the chair?'

'No, I'm good,' I laugh. 'That bench looks a bit uncomfortable.'

Sean fusses round me, finally producing a flask. 'Tea. Proper Tetley's, not that hospital rubbish.' I smile. Suddenly, I'm in love with this crazy man with unruly hair.

I smile up at him, accepting the steaming cup of tea. 'You're so good to me.'

But Sean has become serious. 'Now we're alone . . .'

'What?'

'I need to tell you something important about your past.' I stare at him, puzzled. 'Those odd things you've been seeing—'

'Yeah?'

'Chloe, you're an undercover detective.' The shock of this makes me spit out my tea. It was the last thing I'd expected him to say. 'You were in a car accident while you were trying to get away from somebody who was about to kill you. You work for the Met. Those things the nurse said were your dreams, well, they are real. They're your memories.'

'Memories?'

'The man with the gun who you thought was trying to kidnap you. That guy checking your room. You see, the kidnap really happened and the guy, well, he's someone from the service keeping an eye on you.'

'I don't understand, Sean. If those things are real, why didn't you tell the nurses? Apart from anything else, it means my brain is healing.'

'I can't tell them about those things, and you mustn't either.'

137

'Why, Sean? I don't understand.'

'Your safety depends on it.' I look at him as I try to work out what he is talking about. I instinctively touch my head where my scars are still healing.

'You remember you asked me about a Maria? Well, that was the undercover name you were using at the time of the accident.' I am struggling to take all this in. What does it mean?

'There'll be more memories that come back to you as you get better, but the hospital staff can't know. If they know who you are, it'll put them in danger.'

I stare up at Sean. 'Now you've told me this much, you need to tell me everything.'

'I can't, Chloe, you need to remember for yourself. Otherwise I might be planting false memories.' I try to picture myself as an undercover agent. It seems fantastical.

'What about my colleagues? Surely they'd have come to see me?'

'They think you're still out there, undercover. They don't know about the car crash.'

'This man,' I say. 'What's stopping him from going ahead and kidnapping me? I mean, I'm a sitting target now, aren't I?'

'Remember what I said: you are safe in the hospital. And when they discharge you, we'll go somewhere no one will find you.'

'And the Met?'

'Let's concentrate on getting you better first. We'll cross that bridge when we come to it.'

CHAPTER 55

Adam Coulthard
November 2021

Among Chloe's possessions, I was amazed to find the key to her flat. This was the very piece of the puzzle I needed. Now there would be no doubt at all that this girl was Chloe Seaward.

I knew no one else had come looking for her, and when I entered her flat I saw why: this wasn't a home. There were no personal effects, just boxes piled up against the walls. The post lying on the mat was addressed to Maria Anderson. Was that who she really was? She had asked about a Maria. Anyway, that didn't matter now. I booked a van for the next day and cleared the place out, leaving just the furniture. Just another tenant who'd done a moonlight flit, Maria Anderson had disappeared into the night.

CHAPTER 56

Chloe Seaward
2023

Great, so she was bloody stuck here, passing her time doing nothing but eating and sleeping. Elispeth had told her outright it might be best if she stayed in the cottage and she didn't fancy a walk either. Why didn't they believe her when she told them who she was? She looked at the clock on the bedside table. 5 p.m. — just a bit too early to sleep. On her way downstairs she heard voices. Strange. She was sure no one had knocked, nor had there been the sound of a car on the gravel drive. She stood on the landing, listening.

'You sure Hannah's okay with this?' Elispeth was saying.

'Why wouldn't she be? And anyway, I'm the one leading the investigation.'

'I thought we were keeping her here until the DNA results came back?'

'It's not like I'm planning to leave the country with her. And in any case, the DNA *is* back. Hannah was going through their report when I left.'

'So, is she . . . *her?*' Elispeth said.

Chloe stepped into the kitchen. 'Lisa?'

Lisa smiled at her. 'Chloe, I've come to take you out to dinner to make amends for what we've put you through.'

'In other words you've come to butter me up so I don't complain.' The one person she'd hoped would believe her had pretty much turned her back on her since her arrival.

'I'm so sorry, Chloe, I really am. Look, wouldn't you at least like to get out of here for a bit?'

'Ah, so I'm coming back here again after, am I? You're still keeping me prisoner?'

'They're stressed about the way you managed to find me,' Lisa explained. 'I guess they just want to sort it out.'

'Well, if that's the case I can't see much point in going out.'

'I know you, Chloe. I bet you've been climbing the walls. Come on, let's go out like we used to — you know, get drunk, go a bit wild.'

Chloe laughed, remembering the fun she and Lisa had had back in the day. Going out with Jessica hadn't been the same, and then she was gone too. 'Let me grab my coat.'

As she ran back up the stairs, she heard Lisa call after her, 'Don't be too long, I'm starving.' In her room, she could hear the two of them whispering below. Was this some kind of trap? Maybe it was. Maybe they thought she knew too much and had become a liability to them. Had Lisa been told to get rid of her?

CHAPTER 57

Hannah Littlefair

'Lisa in the loo, is she?' Hannah asked.

'She said she was popping out for a bit,' Georgina said. 'I'm sure she won't be long.'

Selina looked pointedly at her watch. 'I think she's as sick of this place as the rest of us.'

'Well, I hope she won't be. I need to discuss the DNA results with her,' Hannah said.

'Well? Is it her?' Georgina's excitement was palpable.

Hannah sighed. 'There's still no conclusive proof.'

At that moment, Tim burst into the room. 'Kristoff has been seen leaving a house in Moorgate carrying a large holdall.'

'Have we got eyes on him?' Hannah asked.

'Yes, but they're afraid he's about to disappear again.'

'Okay, Tim. My office. We need to get a grip on this situation. The last thing we need is to be caught off guard.' Hannah glanced at the others, who had suddenly become animated again. 'You three stay here and carry on with the imposter case.'

'Don't you need us?' Elliot asked.

'Let's not get ahead of ourselves. We don't know what's happening yet. It might be nothing. He could be off to the launderette — who knows? Oh, and when Lisa reappears, tell her to stay put till I get a chance to speak to her.'

'Okay, Hannah.'

She and Tim went into her office. 'I've put out an alert on all ports, so if he tries to leave the country again, we'll know,' Tim said. Kristoff was a wanted criminal MI5 had an interest in. He was to be watched, but they were in no rush to apprehend the man since they had nothing on him as yet. Hannah had been mightily relieved when he'd left the country — it was one headache less — but just weeks after he stepped on that plane, here he was, back again.

'This house they spotted him leaving, what do we know about it?' she asked.

'Nothing really, boss. Just that he went straight there from the airport and spent the night.'

'Did he have this bag with him when he got off the plane?'

'No, boss. He wasn't carrying any hand luggage and he didn't have any in the hold.'

'Interesting,' Hannah said. 'I wonder where he got it from. He is being followed, isn't he?'

'Yes, ma'am. On foot, and there's a car there too. We're not going to take our eyes off him.'

'Have you informed our friends at MI5?'

'Yes, and they said they're happy for us to continue watching him. They're not sure why he came back yet, as they haven't heard any talk of a possible big operation.'

'In other words, if shit goes down, it's our fault.'

Tim merely smiled.

'Okay, thank you, Tim. Notify the team on the ground that we need to get into that house and find out what's in that bag. Anything changes, let me know at once.'

Tim paused on his way out. 'I overheard you saying something about Chloe. Is there any news?'

'Yes, there is, and it's not exactly the news we were hoping for,' she said.

'Oh?'

'It seems that the DNA sample matches that of someone who was lying in hospital in a coma until a couple of years ago.'

'So it's not Chloe then. That's a relief.'

'They wouldn't commit themselves one way or the other. When I said we'd draw our own conclusions in that case, they warned me not to.'

Tim smiled again. 'They're just trying to cover their arses. Sounds to me like that boyfriend of yours screwed up, and we left Chloe connected to a life-support machine for God knows how long.'

'Then why did the DNA taken from the dead body match with Chloe's?' she demanded.

'But only after extra testing, if I remember rightly,' Tim replied.

'Look, Tim, there's nothing we can do till they give me a straight answer. There's no point getting tied up in endless suppositions. Concentrate on Kristoff for now, and please don't discuss this with the others. All right?'

'Of course. Sorry, boss.' Tim opened the door to reveal Georgina and Selina standing outside, both looking anxious.

'Yes?' Hannah said.

'Sorry, boss. We've just had this odd phone call from Elispeth, and we thought we should speak to you about it.'

'Okay, so what did she say?'

'She says Lisa went to the safe house and took away the imposter.'

Hannah stared at them. 'What?'

'Apparently, she told Elispeth that she was taking the imposter out for a meal. She said she'd cleared it with you, but Elispeth wasn't sure . . .'

Hannah was overcome with a feeling of dread. In return for their permission to bring Jen back here, she'd promised both Max and James that she'd keep her safe. But she had taken her eye off her and now Jen was off God knows where with this woman, probably heading straight into a trap.

'I don't believe this.' Hannah got to her feet. 'Has she gone crazy or something? What exactly did Lisa say to you before she went off?'

'Just that she was going out.' Georgina's voice was shaky.

'I suppose no one thought to ask *where* she was going,' Hannah said.

Georgina stared at her feet. 'No, I didn't think it was important.'

'Oh, you didn't think it was important, did you?' Even as she spoke, Hannah knew she wasn't being fair. She sighed. 'Selina, I need you to contact the team that is watching the house. Someone must have had the sense to follow them.'

'Okay.' Selina turned and fled.

'Georgina, where are you in tracing where this woman came from?'

'I still can't locate her,' Georgina said.

'And Elliot, why didn't he pick this up? He's supposed to be listening to everything that's said in that house.'

'Erm, Hannah . . .' Georgina seemed reluctant to continue. 'Since Lisa is leading this case, well, maybe she has a reason for taking her out.'

'I just worry that she is walking into a trap. Let me try her mobile number.' Hannah picked up her office phone. At least Jen's phone was ringing, but there was no answer.

'Have you tried from your personal phone, boss? Maybe she didn't answer because she didn't recognise the number,' Georgina suggested.

'Good point.' Hannah made the call. She was about to give up when she heard Jen's ringtone, and it was getting closer and closer. Jen had returned, and everything would be sorted. Then Elliot appeared in the doorway, the ringing phone in his hand.

Hannah took the phone from him and stared at it. What was Jen playing at? She could only have left her phone behind on purpose.

CHAPTER 58

Jen Garner

'I owe you an apology.' Jen stole a glance at the woman beside her in the passenger seat. She hadn't said a word since they'd left the safe house. 'It's just that, well, you scared me turning up like that and I panicked. As soon as I realised my mistake—'

'I thought you and I had an unbreakable bond,' the woman said.

'We do. But I believed you were dead. I was just beginning to accept it and getting on with my life, when suddenly you were there, on my doorstep. I just freaked out. I'm sorry.'

'So, you think taking me out for a meal or whatever is going to make everything all right, do you?'

'Yes— I mean no. I just feel so guilty for taking them at their word when they told me you were dead. I couldn't sit in that office any longer knowing it really was you at my door.'

'So, what are you going to do about it? Feeding me isn't going to help, is it?'

'Chloe, if I knew how to make them see, I would. But I can't go against the Met. You know what they're like.'

By now, Jen was just driving. She had no plan for what to do next, except take the imposter away somewhere and get her

146

to open up. Where did she and Chloe go in the good old days? Probably those places didn't even exist anymore. After Brexit and then the pandemic, so many pubs and clubs had closed their doors for good. She couldn't risk taking her to King's Cross in case they were recognised. And what were they going to do tonight? She couldn't take her back to Sam's place. She just needed to give the woman enough rope to hang herself, and then she'd know who she was.

'What about heading toward Leicester Square?' Jen suggested. 'We'll find somewhere to eat and catch up.' Her suggestion was met with silence, so she changed tack. 'I'm curious to know how you managed to find me.'

'Well, we don't have a lot to thank Jessica for, but at least there was that.'

'What do you mean?' Jen asked.

'It was actually through Harry Greenridge. I was out with him and Jessica one night when I happened to run into James.'

'Oh?' Jen remembered Harry Greenridge all right: he was James's former best friend before he was sent down for dealing. She hoped James hadn't been at one of those sex parties Jessica liked so much, or had been buying some of the drugs they dealt.

Chloe smiled faintly. 'You know how it is when you swear you know someone from somewhere but you can't place them?'

'All the time, though in my case it tends to be my kids' friends' parents.' Jen chuckled.

'Well, it was one of those. I thought he might have been someone we'd taken down at some point, so I was, like, really cautious and kept my distance.'

'That couldn't have been easy seeing as you were out as a group.'

'He was such a gentleman,' the woman continued. 'He'd obviously got the impression I was shy, so he kept trying to put me at my ease.' Jen smiled. That was James all over. 'Anyway, I was curious, so I followed him home. That's when I saw you.'

'So much for me disappearing,' Jen replied.

'When I saw the kids, I knew I should get as far away from you as possible in order to keep you safe.'

Jen shook her head. 'If I'd only known . . .'

'Judging by the way you did react, it would hardly have helped, would it?'

'I'm so sorry, Chloe. I mean, it never occurred to me that the DNA tests could have been wrong.'

'Someone certainly cocked up there.' The woman laughed.

'But you're back now, that's all that matters,' Jen said.

How easily they had fallen into their old way of talking. Jen kept having to remind herself that this woman was not her best friend, and her sole purpose in taking her out was to find out who she really was.

CHAPTER 59

Hannah Littlefair

Hannah was barking into the phone while Elliot and Georgina looked on uncomfortably.

'You mean no one followed Lisa when she left the safe house with that woman? . . . I know I told you to watch the bloody house, but didn't you even think why? It was to keep your eyes on the woman, wasn't it, not the architecture. Jesus.' A muffled voice came down the line. 'Yes, I would like you to ring me back with an answer. What d'you think?' She slammed the receiver down and glanced at the two detectives.

'Well, it looks like we'll not be going home anytime soon.'

'Is there anything I can do to help, boss?' Georgina's voice trembled.

'Sorry, Georgina. Elliot.' She sighed. 'We need to make a plan. If someone can get us some drinks, we'll discuss what's to be done.'

As the two younger detectives left the room, Hannah sat slumped in her chair, staring unseeingly at the Long Eaton case file. There were so many things that didn't add up. Who, for example, was this woman who'd been in a coma? The lab

149

had asked her to wait till they'd double-checked their results following this unexpected conclusion. What a fuck-up. What the higher-ups in the Met would say when they found out about this didn't scare her half as much as Max and James's reaction when they found out Jen was missing. Wearily, she pulled out her mobile. She needed to tell Chris that she wasn't going to be home anytime soon.

'Hannah.' He was obviously still half asleep.

'I'm just ringing to let you know I'll be late home. Probably very late.'

'What time is it anyway?' he mumbled.

'About seven, I think.' Hannah looked around for a non-existent clock.

'Is everything okay?' he asked.

'I suppose. Just Jen being Jen.'

He chuckled. 'What's she done now?'

'Not a word about this to anyone, Chris.'

'Hannah, what's happened?' Suddenly he sounded wide awake.

'She's done a runner, taking our imposter with her.'

'What?'

'Our dear Detective Garner has decided that it would be nice to take the imposter out for dinner.'

'Why? What for?'

'Beats me, Chris, but you must keep it to yourself.'

'Of course I will. Anyway, I'm sure Jen won't do anything stupid.'

Hannah sighed. 'That's as may be, but the minute Max or James gets wind of this, I'm in deep shit.'

Chris laughed.

'Chris, it's not funny.'

'You'd better get off the phone and find her, then.'

'Oh, I will. See you if I ever get home. Love you.'

'You too.'

She ended the call and was about to head out the room when her desk phone rang. Without waiting to hear who was calling, she said, 'Please say you've got some good news.'

'Detective Littlefair, it's Commander Conway here.'

'Commander. What can I do for you?'

'I am sorry for the mix-up with the surveillance people. I just wanted to say that we now have two officers tailing Detective Garner.'

'That's excellent news.' *And about time too.*

'Do you wish them to intercept her?'

Hannah considered this for a moment. Should she trust in Jen's instinct, or put an end to this stupid exploit of hers? 'If they can be sure not to lose her, they can follow her for now, unless something untoward happens.'

'Will do, ma'am, and I apologise again for the earlier, erm, miscommunication.'

'No worries. Thank you.'

Well, she'd done it now. Hannah just had to hope that Jen knew what she was doing, and wasn't about to walk into a trap.

CHAPTER 60

Chloe Seaward

She and Lisa were sitting in a pub garden, plates of untouched food in front of them. An awkward silence had fallen — something that had never happened in the old days. Then they'd had almost too much to say, laughing, talking over each other. Happy to be together, Chloe supposed.

Chloe cleared her throat. 'I guess your "happy ever after" worked out okay, then?'

'It was a challenge, what with the kids and all that, but things were going along well until . . . oh, I don't know.' Lisa ran her fingers through her hair.

'Until what?' Chloe asked.

'I guess I . . . You know, you're beginning a new relationship and at first everything is amazing. Then you get to know them, and you begin to see them as they really are. Well, I feel like I've been on a ten-year honeymoon that has just come to an end.'

'James not the man you thought he was?'

'He isn't as accepting of the Met and the things we did.'

'I'm sorry. I hope I wasn't the cause of any issues in your relationship.' Chloe reached out and held Lisa's hand.

'It's not your fault, hun. Maybe I shouldn't have told him about what we did. Anyway, I'm glad you're back. I've missed you. No one could understand me the way you did.'

'The good old days.' Chloe laughed. 'The stuff we used to get up to. My God.'

Lisa giggled. 'Don't remind me.'

'Can't you fix things with James?'

'I hope so, for the children's sake. I guess he needs to realise that the things I got up to were just work. We did them for the service.'

'Remember when we used to tell each other stories about the guys we'd slept with?' Chloe said.

'God, yeah. The ones who passed out as soon as they got to the hotel. And that one lad who turned out to be a virgin.'

'I think he got the hang of it before I sashayed off into the night.' How long had it been since she'd been able to laugh like this?

'So, what about you?' Lisa asked. 'Has there ever been someone important?'

'There was this one guy,' Chloe mused. 'I ended up in a relationship with someone I was tracking. Broke all the rules. He was the first man I'd met who really understood me. I was even prepared to leave the service for him.'

'What happened?'

Chloe shrugged. 'I guess he couldn't give up the drug dealing. So I decided to just disappear.'

'Maybe if you'd spoken to him he might have changed his ways,' Lisa said.

Chloe shook her head. 'I don't believe in happy endings.'

'Like in the movies. Remember that terrible film . . .' They collapsed in mirth. Chloe was beginning to feel like things had returned to how they used to be. She had her best friend back. The only thing she'd ever wanted.

CHAPTER 61

Hannah Littlefair

'Yes, I understand you can't divert your entire team to chasing round London after one of my officers when there is a genuine high-risk individual on the loose. Yes, I am aware that Detective Garner is a highly trained operative with years of experience behind her.' Hannah wished she'd never picked up the bloody phone in the first place. The news of Jen's escapade had reached the higher-ups, and now she was being read the riot act. 'Would you at least consent to my keeping the two officers on her tail, sir? Thank you, sir . . . Yes, my team are keeping a close eye on Kristoff and I will inform you of any developments on that score. Thank you, sir.' Hannah's ears were still ringing with the sound of his voice minutes after she put the phone down. *Typical.* When all they had to do was sit in a bloody field and watch, she was given as many resources as she wanted, but as soon as their imposter was mobile — oh, no. Suddenly, all sorts of questions were asked. You never knew, maybe Jen would end up in the same place as Kristoff and they could kill two birds with one stone. Meanwhile, outside her door, the office was rapidly emptying.

'Tim! Before you go . . .' Hannah called.

'Ma'am?'

'Where are we with Kristoff? And how come everyone is packing up and leaving while we have two active cases on the go?'

'Kristoff has checked into a hotel. Don't worry, he's being watched.'

'Did we get anywhere with the house and what he was carrying in that holdall?'

'No. A couple of our guys went into the house on the pretext of a gas leak and had a look around—'

'And?'

'Nothing, though they didn't question the occupant about Kristoff,' Tim said.

'Who was the occupant? I suppose they did find that out.' Hannah rolled her eyes.

'A single woman.'

'Do we need to bring her in?' Hannah asked.

'I don't see any point. We've run a background check on her, and she has no record, nor any previous connection with Kristoff.' Tim looked pointedly at his watch.

'The thing is, Tim, what's in that bag? Is he moving something, do you suppose?'

Tim shrugged. 'Look, Hannah, we've got people on him, in and outside the hotel. They'll let us know if he so much as sneezes. I expect he's tucked up in bed by now, which is where I ought to be.'

'And while you're getting your beauty sleep, that bag goes off, killing God knows how many people.'

'I really don't see that happening.' By now, Tim was edging towards the door.

'Oh, you don't, do you?'

'But—'

'I've had enough of your casual attitude to your job. Walk out of that bloody door now, and I'm warning you, your security pass won't work tomorrow morning.'

'Hannah!'

'Don't "Hannah" me. You originally wanted to work on the Kristoff case, you swore you wouldn't let him out of your sight. Yet here you are, off home because it's after five.' Even as she spoke, Hannah knew she was going too far. She couldn't afford to lose a second officer when Jen was off who knew where.

'Hannah . . .'

'Don't let the door hit you on the way out, Detective.' Hannah marched back to her office and kicked her door closed. God, that man made her so angry! How the hell had he made it on to this team if he wasn't willing to work late during a major case? She watched him trudge back to his desk and sit down heavily, wondering if he'd still be there after she got back from the meeting room.

When she went in, Georgina, Selina, Ashley and Elliot were all there, working quietly away.

Elliot looked up. 'I know my job's kinda redundant until they return to the safe house, but I thought there might be something else I could do to help.'

'Thank you, Elliot.' What she would have liked would be for him to take over from Tim, so she could get rid of the guy permanently. 'Right, what have we got? First, the DNA from our imposter matched that of a Jane Doe who'd been in hospital in a coma before being discharged two years ago.'

'Is that what the hold-up with the DNA result was all about?' Selina asked.

'Yes. Given the unexpected outcome, they wanted to double-check their findings.'

Selina looked perplexed. 'So, how did she end up as Chloe, then? I don't get it. And why wait two years before identifying herself to us?'

'Assuming this woman is the same as the one we had in the safe house before Lisa saw fit to carry her off, she knows everything about Chloe's past. She couldn't have just woken up with this knowledge.'

'You think someone got to this poor woman and brainwashed her?' Elliot asked.

'I can't think of any other way,' Hannah said. 'Selina, I need you to go undercover at the hospital.'

'Er, okay.' Selina sounded doubtful.

'I think we need to check the staff who were treating her,' Hannah explained.

'I see,' Selina said.

'You'll be a receptionist, so you won't be expected to have any medical knowledge.'

Selina exhaled. 'That's a relief.'

'I want you to talk to the staff on the intensive care ward and see what you can find out about them, and also our Jane Doe. I'll get the background papers emailed over to you as soon as we've finished here.'

Hannah turned to Ashley. 'Tomorrow, I need you to head over to Greenwing Automotive, where Adam works. I know it's not strictly part of this case, but nevertheless it's a bit strange how Adam suddenly went from drug dealing to sales manager. Their HR records haven't told us anything, so someone needs to go there in person.'

'Okay. What am I looking for?' Ashley asked.

'Anything that explains the sudden career change. We also can't ignore the link between Chloe and Adam,' Hannah said.

'Okay, Hannah.'

'Georgina and Elliot. I'd like you both to remain in the office to deal with whatever the other two come up with.'

'Have you had anything back on Lisa and this woman?' Georgina asked.

'We've got someone on their tail. To be honest, I'm torn between dragging them both in and letting it play out.'

'Surely Lisa knows what she's doing,' Selina said.

'God, I hope so.'

CHAPTER 62

Jen Garner

Jen stood at the bar watching the bartender make their cocktails. How easy it was being with this woman, as if the years had slipped away and she was back having fun with her best friend. Her cocktail choices hadn't changed either. She was still drinking Purple Rains like they were going out of fashion. While she waited, Jen looked around to see if she could spot anyone watching them. Hannah would have people on their tail by now.

'Anything else I can get you?' the bartender asked.

'No, that's all, thanks.'

Walking away from the bar, cocktails in hand, she glanced back. He was still watching her.

Her companion grinned. 'I think you've made an impression there, Lisa.'

'Hmm.'

'You've still got it. He stared at you all the way to your seat.'

'Yeah, and I'm old enough to be his mother.'

'I bet you could teach him a thing or two in the bedroom department.'

'Chloe! Anyway, he's much more your type.'

'God no, far too young for me.' They fell about laughing.

'Come on, he'll be thinking we're cougars in a minute,' Jen said.

'I guess neither of us is as young as we used to be.'

Jen gave a wry smile. 'You can say that again.'

'Maybe he likes older women.'

'*Chloe*. If you like him that much, go and chat him up.'

'Nah, I'm out with you tonight.' She winked. 'Anyway, how old is Hannah? She must be loads younger than us.'

'What makes you ask that?' Jen asked.

'Oh, I don't know. She hasn't got the years of service under her belt that we have. To be honest, I can't understand how she landed the job.'

'Well, who else was there? They thought you were dead, and I told them I wasn't interested because of my family.'

'Anyway, I'd rather be out in the field,' the imposter said. 'All that admin. No thanks.'

Everything she said pointed to the fact that this woman was Chloe. No matter how many times Jen tried to trip her up, she hadn't once caught her out. Maybe that was why there was a hold-up with the DNA results — because this really was Chloe. But if that was the case, who was the dead body?

'Fancy going clubbing after this?' The woman's words shattered Jen's contemplation.

'I'm up for it if you are,' Jen said.

'How about that place we always used to go to?'

'Then we'll roll into the office straight from the night-club, just like in the good old days.' Chuckling, Jen pictured Hannah's horrified reaction.

'To Oceana!' The imposter downed her cocktail and stood up. She was surprisingly steady, considering how much they'd had to drink.

'Oceana!' Jen linked arms with her and they marched out of the pub.

CHAPTER 63

Jen Garner

'Wow, this place hasn't changed a bit.' Chloe stood for a moment, gazing around the office. By now, Jen knew without a shadow of a doubt that this woman was Chloe. They'd partied into the morning hours, drinking cocktail after cocktail, and not once had Chloe said or done anything uncharacteristic of her best friend. Every detail had been spot on, right down to the name of their favourite nightclub, which they'd last visited over ten years ago. She knew Hannah would hit the roof, but if this woman was Chloe, they'd treated her abysmally.

Jen watched Chloe make a beeline for her old desk.

'Glad to see they kept it tidy.'

And now for the moment of truth. Hannah flung her door open.

'Lisa! My office. Now!'

Jen made a sheepish face. 'Oops.' Chloe snickered.

In her mind's eye, Jen saw Max standing at his office door with just that look on his face. She steeled herself and went in.

'Han, I can explain—'

'Do you have any idea how much trouble you're in? Without authorisation you've removed a suspect from a safe house—'

'I knew what I was doing—'

'Gallivanted around Central London, where anything could have happened to you—'

'Hannah—'

'I've spent the whole night here at the office making sure you were safe; meanwhile, there's a high-profile criminal on the loose.'

'Hannah, please.'

'Well, out with it, and it had better be good.'

'Since I knew Chloe better than anyone, I thought that if I took her out, you know, got her to relax and let her guard down, she'd let something slip.'

'And? Did she?'

'No, she didn't. Not once.'

'Seeing as she's not Chloe, I find that somewhat surprising,' Hannah said.

Jen frowned. 'Not Chloe? What do you mean?'

'You were in such a rush to conduct your own investigation you didn't think to wait for the DNA test results, did you?' Hannah spat.

Jen looked through the office window at Chloe, who was happily chatting away to Tim, of all people.

'I thought you said there was a problem with the results,' she said.

'Well, Detective Garner, the reason for that was that the DNA sample taken from that woman matched someone who had been in hospital in a coma. So, naturally, they wanted to double-check this rather unexpected result.'

'Shit.' Jen slumped into a chair.

'Still think you know better than the rest of us how to conduct an investigation?'

'So, who is she?' Jen asked.

CHAPTER 64

Hannah Littlefair

Leaving Jen waiting, Hannah picked up the Long Eaton case file and ceremoniously dumped it into her bin. She should never have been persuaded to doubt Chris and his team. They wouldn't have got something that important so wrong. Tim had a lot to answer for.

Finally, she answered Jen's question. 'We don't know who she is. She was in a coma until about two years ago.'

'So, how did she get from coma patient to posing as Chloe Seaward?' Jen asked.

'That's what we're trying to find out,' Hannah replied. 'And there's something else you forgot while you were busy getting pissed with your bosom pal.'

'I'm not sure what you mean,' Jen said.

'Never mind her letting something slip. What information did *you* accidentally disclose?'

'Nothing. We talked about the past.'

'Okay, you need to sit down and prepare a statement. I want everything you spoke about, every word. And I mean everything,' Hannah said.

Jen nodded towards the woman out in the main office. 'What's going to happen to her?'

'I'm not sure. Right now we've got her exactly where we want her. I want to remind you that for the duration of this case you're to be referred to as Lisa Carter, and you're only to respond to that name. Got it?'

'Yes.'

'My old desk is free. Use that, and here're your login details.' Hannah handed Jen a slip of paper.

Jen sighed. 'I guess I'm off the case now. Hannah, I'm sorry.'

Hannah said nothing. She hadn't yet decided whether or not to take Jen off the case. Though it would be difficult to keep her on, given what had just happened. Meanwhile, what to do with the imposter? There were active cases running that would need to be discussed, and reports lying around. They dealt daily with information covered by the Official Secrets Act. Who knew what this woman was up to?

CHAPTER 65

Chloe Seaward

After so long out in the cold, Chloe was home at last, back in the familiar office. She couldn't believe how little had changed. Apart from the odd new face dotted about, even the people were the same. Idly, she tapped at the keyboard on her desk, hoping something might appear on the screen. Where the hell was the actual computer? Networked, she supposed, all operating via some cloud or other. Finally, she had made it to the very heart of the service, and its vast reserve of information. After all, this was the reason why she'd gone to Lisa's in the first place. She just needed a password . . .

Through Hannah's office window she could see Lisa clearly receiving a dressing-down.

The Lisa who left Hannah's office wasn't the Lisa she had been out partying with a few hours ago.

'Are you all right?' Chloe asked.

Lisa shrugged. 'Just had the book thrown at me, haven't I? I'll get over it.'

'You seem a bit distant.'

'I'm fine, honestly. Just not used to being told off like that,' Lisa said.

Chloe shook her head. 'It's not fair. It's not like you did anything wrong.'

'I should have followed the regulations, and not broken you out.'

'You didn't break me out. Look, why don't we get away from here? We were perfectly fine when we were out. It'll cheer you up.' Her search could wait; she was finally at the epicentre. And she might need Lisa.

'I wish. Gotta work unfortunately.' Lisa made for one of the desks.

'Pity.' Seeing that Lisa was already typing away, Chloe sat back and concentrated on trying to listen in to what the others were saying, and what they were working on.

CHAPTER 66

Adam Coulthard
2023

It took a lot of perseverance, but finally it paid off. I had found my perfect subject and began systematically turning her into another Chloe. I fed her the details of Chloe's past: the people she'd worked with, the cases she'd been involved in. I gave her Lisa Carter's address, and told her stories of her and Lisa's exploits. We worked on getting her fit. Our sex life was better than it had been with the real Chloe.

But once I had crafted my perfect woman, I began to get bored with her. Needing something to do outside the home, I looked for a job. I knew I was clever. After all, I'd sold drugs for a living, made a mint at it and had never been caught. After a lot of searching, I happened upon a job with an up and coming "green" car-manufacturing firm. Somehow I managed to convince them that I was the real deal and they offered me the job. The only problem was it meant moving to Reading.

Wanting to be free of Chloe, I found excuses to criticise her, accused her of things she hadn't done. After one almighty row, I walked out. After the things I'd said, there was no way she'd come looking for me.

CHAPTER 67

Selina
Chessington Hospital

Selina went to the reception desk of the intensive care unit and introduced herself. 'Hi, I'm Katya, the temp from Ownhaven.'

'Am I pleased to see you!' the nurse said. 'We've been begging them to send us a replacement for months.'

Selina smiled. 'Well, I'm glad I've made someone's day.'

'Come on through.' The nurse got up, went to the doors leading into the ward and pressed a code on the intercom. 'We don't want people wandering in and out who shouldn't be here,' she explained.

'I guess you don't.'

The nurse eyed the young woman doubtfully. 'You seem a bit young. I hope you won't find it too quiet for you here.'

'I like a bit of peace. It'll be nice to be away from the hustle and bustle,' Selina said.

The nurse smiled. 'You'll love it here then. I'll take you to the staffroom and show you where you can leave your things.'

She ushered Selina to a room off a corridor that ended in another set of doors. 'Here we are. Oh, and Dr Shanty is here, so you can meet him.'

The man held out his hand.

'Dr Shanty is from the neurology department. He's our senior medical advisor,' the nurse said.

'Pleased to meet you.'

'One reason why it's so quiet is that a number of the patients here are in a coma. It's my job to look after these cases,' Dr Shanty said.

'Oh, I see,' Selina repeated.

'We have a wonderful team of nurses who take care of them, Mabel being one of them.' The nurse blushed. 'I generally come down twice a day to see how the patients are progressing.'

'How many staff are on this ward?' Selina asked.

'We currently have three coma patients. Each has their own nurse who works a twelve-hour shift. Mabel here is the sister in charge of the ward, and is on hand if any of them need assistance,' the doctor explained.

'Are the patients allowed visitors?'

'Only the coma patients,' he said. 'Their families tend to come every day to sit with them.'

'They're a lovely bunch,' Mabel added. 'I'm sure you'll get to know them in no time.'

'I understand I will also be responsible for typing up the patients' notes,' Selina said. 'Is that right?'

'Yes. The doctors generally record their observations into a Dictaphone — I hope you're a trained audio typist.' Mabel shook her head. 'The last person we had was hopeless.'

'Oh yes, I am.'

'Well, that's good.' Mabel opened one of the lockers. 'You can use this to keep your things in, then I'll take you round to meet everyone.'

Selina did as she was told. Nurse Mabel seemed nice, so did the doctor. She had a feeling she'd get along just fine.

CHAPTER 68

Adam Coultyard
Greenwing Automotive

About to go into his office, Adam turned towards the pretty young receptionist, who was calling to him from the end of the corridor. 'Where's the fire?'

'I've brought your new starter.' She blushed as he eyed her up and down.

'New starter?' he asked.

'The new recruit for the sales team. You've forgotten all about it, haven't you?'

'No, Kim, I haven't forgotten. I just wasn't expecting him so soon.'

'Benji is joining us fresh out of university,' Kim said.

'Oh, okay.' Adam turned to the young man. 'Full of bright ideas then, I hope.'

'Yes, sir,' Ashley said.

'Less of the "sir". It's Adam.' He held out his hand. 'You've got a firm handshake there, Benji. That's good. Why don't we go into my office and I'll sort out where you can start.' Adam showed Ashley into a plush office full of the latest hi-tech equipment.

169

'See you later, Benji.' Kim turned and headed off.

'Like I said, I wasn't expecting you to turn up today, so I'll have to think where I can put you. I'm sure we'll fit you in somewhere; there's certainly plenty to be done.' Adam laughed.

Inside, Ashley viewed the various gadgets in awe. Adam picked up an iPad that was lying on the desk. 'Just catching up on *Stranger Things*. You a fan, Benji?'

Ashley shook his head apologetically. 'My kid sister watches it. It's a bit gory for my taste.'

Looking slightly disappointed, Adam laid the tablet aside. 'Now, where to put you?'

'Anywhere's okay with me.'

'Let's start with a tour of the factory, shall we? Then we'll take it from there.'

'Great,' Ashley said. 'I can't wait to get started.'

Adam smiled. 'Like the enthusiastic attitude, Benji. Maybe you can bring a fresh perspective — the automotive industry is facing tough times, what with all the new environmental regulations coming into force.'

'Green energy is the way to go, Adam,' Ashley said.

'Indeed.' Adam didn't attempt to hide his lack of enthusiasm. 'Anyway, let me take you round and I'll show you how a green car is manufactured.'

CHAPTER 69

Hannah Littlefair

'It looks like this case is moving in a new direction,' Hannah announced to her team. 'You cannot have failed to notice that our imposter is now installed in the office.'

'Why's that?' Georgina asked. 'Something going off, is it?'

'Lisa decided she really is Chloe,' Hannah said, 'so she thought she ought to be returned to the fold.'

Georgina was clearly on tenterhooks. 'So, who is she?'

Hannah changed the subject. 'Have you heard from either of the others yet?'

'Just that they're both in place,' Elliot said.

'Good. Meanwhile, I've got Lisa preparing a report of her findings from the conversations she had with the supposed Chloe.'

'She off the case now, is she?' Georgina said.

'I haven't decided. The woman's presence here is rather awkward since she's not yet been definitively identified. Meanwhile, there are active investigations running, and if she isn't Chloe, she could be spying on us.' Hannah was at a loss as to how to play this. She needed Jen's help, since she knew

more about the real Chloe than any of them. It was also possible that Jen herself was the target of the imposter. For this
reason, she wanted to keep them both close.

'Hannah,' Elliot said, 'suppose you sent Lisa and this
woman out into the field? You know, to keep an eye on
Kristoff or something? That way they'll be out of the office.'

Hannah shook her head. 'I'm not sure that's a good idea,
Elliot. Anyway, we already have people tracking Kristoff.'

'That's the point,' Elliot explained. 'Those people can
also keep an eye on Lisa and the woman.'

'Plus, if she's leading Lisa into a trap, she's more likely to
do it out there than in the office,' Georgina added. 'We'll be
giving her enough rope to hang herself.'

Elliot nodded. 'Force her to act, instead of having her
wait around here for months.'

'Hmm. That might be an idea,' Hannah said. 'In fact,
let's do it. Good thinking, Elliot.' She headed for her office,
wishing again that she could replace Tim with this young man.

CHAPTER 70

Jen Garner

Despite what Hannah had said about the DNA test, Jen was finding it hard to believe that this woman wasn't the real Chloe. She knew so much, down to the smallest detail. Across the room from where she sat, Chloe was moving among the others as if she were one of them, as if she belonged. Oh, what was the point? It was all but confirmed Jen was off the case anyway, so why keep going round and round in circles?

As she sat working on her statement, she noticed Tim making his way to Hannah's office, where she could see him arguing with her. Soon afterwards, her desk phone rang, and Hannah summoned her. Tim was just leaving as Jen reached the office door, his furious expression directed at her as they passed each other.

So much for Hannah being a friend as well as a boss. She was nothing but a boss as she told Jen curtly to sit down.

'The Kristoff case,' Hannah began. 'Tim has agreed that you and Chloe can join the team that is tracking him.'

'So I'm definitely off the Chloe case then,' Jen said.

'Not exactly. The thing is, we need this woman out of this office until we know who sent her, and why. So I'm sending the two of you out into the field together,' Hannah explained.

'Okay.'

'That way she's not picking up any information about our active cases and you will be able to watch her.'

'What if I'm the target?' Jen said.

'There is a team watching Kristoff. They can watch you at the same time.'

'Sounds like a plan.'

'It means that Tim will be your supervisor. Is that a problem for you?'

'No, I'm good with it,' Jen said. 'Though I'm not so sure about Tim.'

From the look he'd given her just now, it certainly wasn't fine with him. For her part, she hated the guy, but if it meant being with Chloe, she'd deal with it.

CHAPTER 71

Chloe Seaward

Chloe looked up to see Lisa standing beside her desk. 'Everything okay?'

'We've been assigned a case,' Lisa said. 'We're to track a wanted criminal who has just turned up in London.'

'How come? Does that mean they believe me? Am I back?'

'Looks like I've managed to convince them.' Lisa smiled. 'I told them how much you remembered about us.'

'What happened with the DNA results? They must have come back positive then,' Chloe said.

'I'm not sure.' Lisa sounded vague.

'Well, when do we get started?' Chloe stood up and brushed herself down, ready for action.

'Tim is finalising everything with Hannah now. It's his case, so we'll be working under him,' Lisa said.

'Okay, so when do I get to pick up my equipment?'

'I don't think they're going to allow you to go running around London armed just yet. They're not letting me have mine back either.'

'Oh, okay.' She sort of understood. Plus, there was the small matter of the weapon she'd left behind when she came back. 'I suppose Tim will let us know when he wants us to start.'

'Yeah, I'm sure he'll *summon* us when he's ready.' Lisa made no attempt to hide her bitterness.

'You two still not getting on?' Chloe asked.

'Let's just say he doesn't like me very much, and the feeling is mutual.' Lisa turned away. 'Now, I need to finish this statement for Hannah.'

'Well, at least you've got access to the system. I'm still waiting for a response from IT. Seems they had written me off as dead, like everyone else.' Chloe wondered about the girl who'd been mistaken for her. Who was she, and why did she die?

CHAPTER 72

Selina
Chessington Hospital

Mabel led "Katya" back to the reception desk.

'It really is silent, isn't it?' Selina said. 'I expected to hear the monitors beeping and all that.'

'You only hear those sounds when you're inside the ward,' Mabel explained.

'I guess the only people I'll be dealing with are the visitors.'

The nurse nodded. 'Yes, you'll get to know all of them in no time.'

'Great. I'd better get started then. I suppose I'll need a password or something to get into the computer.'

'Yes, that's being arranged. Meanwhile, make yourself at home and I'll come and check on you in a bit.'

'Okay. Maybe I'll give this desk a bit of a tidy up.' Selina was itching to have a good nose around. This was sure going to be different from her usual workplace, with its constant air of high drama. She sat on the swivel chair and spun it around, then began to root around in the desk drawers.

When visiting hour began, Mabel stood beside her to help her book them in. That done, Selina decided to go for a wander around the ward. Her password hadn't yet arrived, and she was bored with sitting at the desk moving paperclips . She went into the ward, passing rooms where people sat holding the hands of their loved ones. In one room, obviously that of a coma patient, a young man sat working on a laptop. Every bay had a nurse seated just inside, who waved to her or nodded as she passed. The atmosphere was hushed, with only the beeping of the monitors to break the silence.

'They look so peaceful,' she whispered to one of the nurses.

He smiled. 'Just like they're asleep.'

In another bay people stood hugging one another, some crying. 'What's going on?' Selina asked.

'She's just been placed in a medically induced coma,' the nurse said.

'What does that mean?'

'It means the doctors have deliberately caused her to remain unconscious.'

Selina was shocked. 'Why would they do that?'

'They often do it to give their bodies time to heal.'

'So, how long will they remain like that?'

'It depends. The doctors keep a constant check on them, measure the brain's responses and all that. They have often had major brain surgery, so it needs time to heal.'

'Poor girl. I hope she's woken up soon.'

'This one's likely to be in for the long haul, I'm afraid,' he said. 'By the way, I'm Nurse Millington.'

'Katya. Pleased to meet you. I'm the new receptionist.'

'I know. I saw you being shown round earlier.'

'No wonder you didn't ask what I was doing here.'

He laughed. 'You didn't look too dangerous.'

'Later.' She tossed her hair as she turned and walked away.

CHAPTER 73

Jen Garner

Tim was briefing Jen and Chloe as a 3D version of the city was displayed on the meeting table in front of them. 'Our target is in the Micro Hotel, which is situated here.' He jabbed a stubby finger at the map. 'We've got units placed here, here, here and here.'

'Meaning you've got all exits covered.' Chloe rolled her eyes. 'So why not just bust in there and arrest him?'

Jen was beginning to like this new Chloe more and more. She wasn't taking any shit from Tim.

'We're playing a long game. We have to know what he's up to before we can apprehend him,' Tim replied.

Chloe nodded. 'I guess the bosses are hoping he'll lead us to the big guys.'

'What's he done so far?' Jen questioned.

'Not a lot,' Tim said. 'He spent the night before last in the house of a woman who isn't known to us, leaving with a mystery holdall that he didn't arrive with, then went straight from there to the hotel, where he spent last night.'

'The woman checks out, right?' Jen was growing impatient with Tim's officious tone.

179

'Apparently, she is a city council office worker with no known links to organised crime.'

'There must be a reason for him staying with her though,' Jen persisted.

But Tim didn't respond. 'What I need you two to do is track him on foot as soon as he leaves the hotel.'

Chloe giggled. 'Good job I didn't put my heels on today.'

'And is Kristoff aware that he's being followed?' Jen asked.

'I'm pretty sure he knows.'

She frowned. 'But if he knows, he's not going to show himself, is he? How long are we prepared to wait it out?'

Tim cleared his throat. 'There is always a chance that he might try to get past us.'

'Right, Lisa, we'd better get ready to roll.' Chloe was obviously forestalling the brewing argument.

'The minute he leaves his room, we'll get our people in. They'll bug the place, and if he's left the bag behind, they'll be able to see what's in it.'

CHAPTER 74

Chloe Seaward

They were sat in a random car park waiting for Tim to tell them when Kristoff had left the hotel. Lisa seemed quiet, staring into space, and Chloe couldn't help but fiddle with her earpiece. She hadn't worn one in so long, she wasn't used to them, or maybe they'd changed.

'You get used to it after a while,' Lisa said, turning her attention back to her.

'Please tell me they never used to be this uncomfortable?'

'No, they've definitely changed. I know when I came back to the service, I couldn't believe we no longer needed to have something attached to us to pick up chatter.'

'I guess technology has moved on, though I certainly don't miss the wires we used to wear.' Chloe laughed, and Lisa eventually joined in. Something wasn't right. Lisa seemed distant today and not so pally and friendly. 'You okay? You seem rather quiet?' Chloe asked, 'I hope I've not done something wrong?'

'Na, I'm good. Just think we're wasting our time. But hey, what do I know?'

181

'It beats sitting in the office though, trying to log in to those damn computers. I even tried to get onto the screen in the boardroom with no luck.'

'You still not able to get back in?'

'Ha, no, I think they've deleted my existence.' Chloe laughed, though she really couldn't understand why she couldn't get into the damn computer, or why IT weren't returning her calls, or even why they'd deleted her in the first place. Then again, they'd thought she was dead, so what did she expect? At least they were all more accepting of her now. Even if she didn't have the computer access, she was back on the streets tracking a criminal.

'Lisa, Chloe, your target is on the move.' Tim's voice came into their ears, almost like he was sat in the car with them.

'Here we go.' Lisa suddenly seemed to come to life and was ready to roll.

'Just like old times,' Chloe replied, getting out of the car. 'How far is it from here?'

'I think we're pretty close. Tim seemed to think we'd intercept Kristoff as he walked past.'

'Standing on corners like the good old days.' She laughed.

'You going to be okay following from the opposite side of the road if I follow from behind?' Lisa asked.

'Yeah, or I can go behind, whatever is easiest.'

'Okay, let's go with that then,' Lisa said, and they both walked towards the intercept point.

Chloe started to feel butterflies in her stomach and couldn't understand why on earth she was feeling so nervous; she had done this thousands of times before and she was back with her best friend by her side.

'To control, Chloe is following our suspect from behind and I'm attempting to follow from the other side of the street, over,' came Lisa's voice through her ear. She didn't have to wait for long before their target appeared and Chloe slowed her pace, trying to not make it obvious that she was following him, glancing across the road to check Lisa was still there.

Suspect intercepted on the corner of Cardigan Road

The whole situation felt alien to her as she continued to follow this person through the streets of London. She shouldn't be feeling this way; she'd done it dozens of times in the past — maybe she was just out of practice? As they continued along the road, Lisa's voice echoed in her ear.

Suspect passing Willow Street on the left, continuing on

Chloe knew she should pay attention to what was going on ahead, because if he stopped, then she risked overtaking him and losing him completely. Luckily for her, he just kept on walking, seemingly unconcerned with what was going on around him.

She knew Lisa thought this was just a waste of time and energy when there were three cars following anyway, so why did Tim want them out on foot as well? Unless this was just a way to get them out of the office? Or was she just feeling paranoid given that it had taken them so long to accept that she was Chloe Seaward and not some master criminal?

Suspect crossing Cardigan Road and turning down Evermore Road to the right

'Target is slowing down,' came the message in her ear, breaking her out of her daydream. She hoped that something wasn't about to happen right in front of her.

Unknown female walking towards suspect, body language suggests known to each other

Maybe they were going to get some action, as Kristoff stopped and greeted the unknown female.

Unknown female embrace with suspect

Shit, she couldn't just stop still on the street and wait for the suspect to continue on with his journey. She regretted not paying better attention to what was going on in front of her, or she could've taken action before it was too late.

Officer compromised

'Dammit, game over,' she muttered to herself, as she walked past the suspect and his female companion, who had started checking out each other's tonsils.

'Chloe, make your way to Gold Rush Road on the right and a car will pick you up.'

She didn't bother acknowledging the instruction. She glanced over to where Lisa had stopped and was searching for something in her bag.

Suspect and unknown female stopped and engaged in kissing

Making her way to Gold Rush Road, she glanced back one more time to check on her friend.

Suspect and unknown female continuing along Evermore Road

Turning onto Gold Rush Road, she saw the car and jumped in.

'Take me round the block and get me back behind them,' she shouted.

'I'm afraid I can't, officer, I'm under strict instructions to return you to the office.'

'Goddamn it,' Chloe shouted, hitting the back of the head-rest in front of her. 'Tim, whatever your name is,' she continued to shout to no response in her ear other than Lisa's continued tracking commands.

Turning left onto Closure Street

'I'm sorry, officer, but my instruction is to return you to the office.'

CHAPTER 75

Jen Garner

Chloe had just proven right there in front of her that she wasn't the real Chloe because the real Chloe wouldn't make such a rookie mistake.

Continuing along Closure Street

She didn't have time to think about that now. She was the only one left following Kristoff on foot, unless they were about to put someone in her place.

Suspect passing Cowboy Street on the left

God dammit, he was leading them around the block back to the hotel with his mystery female companion, and their hand holding and laughing confirmed what they were going back there for.

Suspect turning back onto Cardigan Road

She would have serious words with Tim and Hannah when she made it back to the office. She was freezing and her feet were cold.

'Do we have an identity of the female?' Jen asked impatiently, as she continued to follow on the opposite side of the road. By now her hands were freezing and she could hardly feel her feet.

'Negative,' came the response from Tim in her ear.

'Hadn't we better get someone on that sharpish before we lose them back into the hotel?'

'Working on it, Detective, you just continue with what you're doing.'

Passing Willow Street on the right

This was stupid. She might as well just give up on the surveillance right now.

Suspect and unknown female entering Micro Hotel

'Thank you, officer, take the next right and the car will be there to return you to the office.' What a waste of a productive afternoon following a wanted criminal picking up a hooker. They could've been sat in the office trying to figure out where Chloe had come from and who had sent her, but no. She'd have Tim for this.

'Please tell me you got something from his hotel,' Jen asked to complete silence.

* * *

Back in the flat that night, Jen busied herself with making dinner, while reassuring Chloe that her mistake wasn't important. It had all been a giant waste of time anyway, she said, and she'd make sure Hannah knew about it tomorrow. Chloe had finally been given a password to the public access part of the computer system, so she was somewhat mollified.

186

CHAPTER 76

Selina
Chessington Hospital

Selina went into the staffroom to put her things in her locker and found Dr Shanty getting himself a cup of tea. He smiled at her. 'Hi, Katya. Back for more?'

'Of course.' Selina grinned. He wasn't that bad-looking, actually. Maybe if she flirted with him a bit, she might get some information out of him. 'Get up to much last night?'

'No time to be getting up to anything,' he said. 'My life's all work and study.'

She laughed. 'Sounds like mine. What are you studying? I thought you were a highly qualified neuro . . . neuro something.'

'Neurologist.' His mouth cracked into an amused smile. 'Not highly qualified enough, unfortunately.'

'Shows what I know,' Selina said. 'Patients still all asleep, then?'

He nodded. 'Sound asleep.'

'It must be hard for their relatives,'

'It is. I remember the husband of one of the patients who spent all day, every day, at his wife's bedside, waiting for her to wake up.'

'Ah. How romantic.'

Dr Shanty chuckled. 'Well, at least she wasn't nagging him or answering back.'

'Ooh, go on. Though it's true I'm a sucker for a love story,' Selina said.

'I'll make sure someone lets you know if I ever fall into a coma,' he said.

'You do that.' She left the room, still laughing to herself as she headed down the corridor. Hopefully, they'd have her password for her today. She sat down at the desk she'd spent hours tidying the day before and eyed the mess. What on earth went on at night? Amid the bits of paper and Post-it notes she found a memo with her login details. Great. Now she could get down to doing what she'd been sent here for.

Mabel poked her head around the door. 'Morning, Katya.'

'Morning, Mabel. Any new patients come in overnight?'

'None, dear, and we're not expecting any up from surgery today, though you never know about A & E. Can I bring you a hot drink? I'm just about to make one.'

'Thank you, Mabel. That would be wonderful.'

CHAPTER 77

Ashley
Greenwing Automotive

With a cheery wave at Kim, Ashley walked past the reception desk. He and Adam had been in Adam's office till late, brainstorming ways to increase sales, which had taken a lot of bullshitting on Ashley's part. Adam seemed okay as a boss, though Ashley was yet to find out how he'd managed to get himself appointed manager.

As he reached the office door, he waited, as he was sure he could hear giggling coming from the other side and didn't just want to barge in on his second day. So he waited for a moment, composed himself and knocked.

The giggling seemed to stop suddenly, and Ashley was about to knock again when the door opened and two women made their way out of the office — the blonde one yanking her short skirt down and the second looking like she'd just got changed in a hurry but giving him an alluring look all the same.

'Come in,' Adam shouted from the other side of the door.

'Morning, boss,' Ashley said as he walked into the room, sensing exactly what had just been going on.

189

'And a good morning to you,' Adam responded, standing up and adjusting himself.

'I hope I didn't disturb anything?'

'No, no, my secretaries were just leaving.' *Is that what they call them these days?* Ashley thought to himself as he took a seat on the opposite side of the desk, immediately wondering what might have been happening moments before in the same space.

'Get up to much last night?' he asked.

'Not really. Telly and a takeaway. So much for the bachelor lifestyle.' Adam laughed. 'How about you?'

'About the same, though I didn't sleep a wink; my head was buzzing with ideas for this place.'

Adam yawned, looking thoroughly disinterested. 'Good to hear. Anyway, let me get us a coffee and then we can get started.'

After Adam had left the room, Ashley sat for a moment or two, staring at the empty desk. How long did it take someone to make a cup of coffee? Two minutes? Five? He didn't want to be caught snooping, but he might not get another chance. Ashley dashed around to the other side of the desk and began pulling out the drawers. He found nothing but a pair of shoes, a packet of condoms and chewing gum. Didn't Adam do any work? The computer, of course, asked him for a password. He tried *Chloe* just in case, but it wasn't that. Then he heard a noise at the door, and just made it to his own chair before Adam came in.

'Two coffees,' Adam said. 'So, about these ideas of yours, Benji, my boy.'

CHAPTER 78

Jen Garner

They were both already in the office when Hannah marched in, stopping first at Chloe's desk. 'Tim says everything went according to plan yesterday?' Hannah looked promptly at Jen as she spat out her tea, then moved over towards her desk.

'Everything okay, Lisa?'

'I'm not sure which part of the whole charade Tim thought was a success—' Hannah raised her hand, cutting Jen off mid flow.

'Lisa, our weekly feedback meeting will be in room forty-four at around ten. Try and be there on time.'

'Of course, boss.'

'And Chloe, go and see Tim and ask him if he needs you to do anything.'

'Of course. Yesterday was pretty much a write-off—'

Hannah cut her short. 'Now, if you don't mind.'

'Okay, Hannah.'

Chloe watched Hannah stride off and turned to Jen. 'Oh, how I don't miss those meetings.'

'I wish I could miss this one,' Jen muttered. Who knew, maybe Chloe and Tim would get on like a house on fire.

* * *

Coffee in hand, Jen walked into room forty-four, still annoyed at their wasted day following Kristoff. The sooner he got off British soil the better. Let someone else deal with him. She sat down in a free chair and looked expectantly at her boss.

'Chloe with Tim, is she?' Hannah asked. She began handing out iPads to the gathered team.

Jen switched on the tablet. 'Yep, delivered her there myself.'

'Right. We'll begin with Jen's assignment with Chloe yesterday.'

'She made a crucial mistake while we were tailing Kristoff,' Jen said. 'The Chloe I knew would never have made such a basic error.'

'Our officer at Chessington Hospital has nothing to report as yet,' Georgina said.

'Did she at least get a feel for the place?' Jen asked.

'She said that the security is top-of-the-range. No one gets access to the ward without authorisation.'

'And what about tracing where the imposter came from?' Hannah said.

'I'm still having no luck. She seems to have materialised out of nowhere.' Georgina laughed nervously.

Hannah frowned. 'Well, she must have come from somewhere. Keep at it, Georgina. How's Ashley doing at Greenwing Automotive?'

'Ashley was given a tour of the building. He reports that the operations there are fully automated but has yet to find out anything about Adam,' Elliot responded.

'Nothing at all?' Jen asked.

'No, not really. Just that Adam didn't seem keen on having a new assistant. Which could indicate that he didn't want anyone learning too much about him.'

'Hannah, what did the psychologist say about planting memories into someone with amnesia?'

'He said it would be possible that this woman really does think she is Chloe. But we could do her harm by showing her that she is mistaken about her identity. It could cause a mental breakdown.'

'I can see that,' Jen said. 'I wouldn't want to wake up tomorrow and be told everything I knew about myself was a lie.' As soon as the words were out of her mouth, she realised that this was what she'd done to James — well, not exactly, because he'd been lied to about *her*, not himself. Still, it must have done him harm. To all intents and purposes, he was living with a stranger.

Suddenly, the door to room forty-four burst open.

CHAPTER 79

Chloe Seaward

Chloe marched in waving one of the tablets. 'Why are you investigating Sean?'

'What do you think you're doing barging in like this?' Hannah demanded. 'Out! This minute.'

'No, hang on,' Lisa said. 'What did you just say?'

'I *said*, why are you watching Sean.' Chloe pointed at the photo on her screen. 'That's Sean, my husband. He took care of me when I was in hospital, he helped me get better.'

'You're saying that person is called Sean?' Hannah asked.

'Yeah. We were married. I could hardly mistake him for someone else.'

'Lisa, take Chloe to my office and wait for me there,' Hannah ordered.

Lisa stood up and went over to her, but Chloe shook her off. 'No. I want to know what's going on.'

'We are investigating his business affairs,' Hannah said. 'I called this meeting without you, because you were closely involved with A— I mean Sean.'

'Okay, okay. Have it your own way.' Chloe left the room with Lisa.

Outside in the corridor, Lisa buttonholed her. 'How come you didn't tell me about Sean?'

'It was over long ago, so it didn't seem relevant.'

'So you must have known he was a drug dealer, then.'

'What?' This was total rubbish. Sean was just a sweet man that she had fallen in love with. He certainly wasn't into drugs. Sure, he'd hurt her, but she couldn't let him go down for something he hadn't done.

CHAPTER 80

Hannah Littlefair

'Was I imagining things, or did Chloe just march in here with a photo of her ex-husband and demand to know why we were looking into someone called Sean?'

'Yep,' Georgina said. 'She was pretty angry about it too.'

'Phew. For a minute there, I thought I'd gone off my head,' Hannah said.

'But what do we do about it, boss? Do we tell her?'

'We'll have to be careful how we handle it,' Hannah replied. 'We don't want her having a complete mental breakdown, do we? I'd better get in touch with Dr Spellbound.'

* * *

Hannah ended the meeting and returned to her office, still unsure as to what to say to "Chloe".

The imposter, her face a picture of confusion, stood as soon as Hannah opened the door. 'I don't understand what's going on. You said you're investigating Sean's business affairs.'

'That's right,' Hannah replied. 'Was Sean working at the automotive company when you met him?'

'No.'

'So, what was he doing then?'

'I don't know exactly,' Chloe said, 'just that he quit his job to look after me.'

'That was good of him. Why was he looking after you? Were you ill?'

'I was in hospital after a car accident. I was in a coma actually.'

There was a shocked silence for a few moments while Hannah and Jen took in this revelation. They'd known all along that this woman had awoken in hospital after an accident two years ago, but they'd never considered the possibility that the real Chloe Seaward could have been the mysterious coma patient. Hannah couldn't see how else she would know Adam. But again, what about the DNA . . . ? Her head felt primed to explode.

Lisa cleared her throat. 'I think I heard you say you were married to him, is that right?'

'Yes, I was,' Chloe said.

'And are you still married?' Lisa asked.

'Well, no, we separated. Look, why don't I try and get hold of him, and we can sort this out.'

'Sorry, Chloe, but you can't do that. It's an ongoing investigation and you're involved with him.'

'But I can help you. I can go and see him, pretend that I want to get back together with him. I can get you all the information you need.'

'Sorry, Chloe, but that won't work. Go home with Lisa now and I'll be in touch.'

Chloe glared at her for a moment, and then turned and walked away.

CHAPTER 81

Selina
Chessington Hospital

Finally, Selina had access to the patients' records and could get on with what she'd been sent here to do. She found Chloe's notes almost at once. Selina winced as she read through the injuries Chloe had sustained — it was a miracle she'd survived at all. Following brain surgery, Chloe had been placed in an induced coma to allow the lesions to heal. Fine, but the medical record couldn't tell her anything about what they really wanted to know, not even where she was headed when her car went through that crash barrier.

'Coffee time!' With a start, Selina quit the program.

'Sorry, dear.' Mabel put a mug down on the desk. 'Didn't mean to make you jump.'

Selina laughed. 'I was miles away. Thank you for the coffee, I was dying for a cup.' She took a swig and tried not to grimace. Mabel's coffee was always half cold.

Mabel grinned. 'I'm trying to butter you up so you'll stick around. I'm not the only one either. Dr Shanty seems to have taken quite a shine to you.'

Selina blushed. 'He seems nice.'

'He's a good man,' Mabel said. 'Anyway, can't stand here gossiping, I've the ward rounds to do.'

* * *

Soon after Mabel had left, visiting hour began. As she booked them in, Selina wondered how some random stranger had been able to gain access to a coma patient. Chloe's notes stated that she had arrived alone following a crash in early November 2021 and had received no visitors for the first couple of days until her husband — a man named as Sean Sterling — arrived. A week or so after that, Chloe started to regain consciousness. Here's where the notes became interesting:

> *Patient asks about someone called Maria. Neither she nor her husband know anyone of that name. Patient is moving into the post-traumatic amnesia recovery period.*

Could Chloe's real name be Maria? Had it been her husband who convinced her that her name was Chloe Seaward? After all, the hospital staff would have no reason to question what her husband was telling them.

Selina read on to the next note of interest, dated a week later:

> *Patient suffers her first post-traumatic hallucination; she is convinced that there is a strange man on the ward, who keeps looking into her bay. Suffers a panic attack. No medication required as patient is calmed by her husband.*
>
> *NOTE: No unauthorised person has come into the ward.*

She wondered if this Sean had gained access to Chloe on the pretext of being her husband. Could this woman be the real Chloe? She needed more information on the car accident, and especially this supposed husband's background and history. Reading on, she learned that Chloe had been discharged into her husband's care, having regained the use of her legs. She sent this information in an email to her boss, asking her to check out who Sean Sterling was.

CHAPTER 82

Jen Garner

As they walked outside, Jen grabbed Chloe's arm. 'How come you never said anything about Sean, especially since you were married to the guy?' she asked again. 'We stayed up all night talking about the good old days and you never mentioned a thing.'

'I didn't think it was relevant since he came on the scene later,' Chloe said.

'It was just a shock, that's all. It's not every day a detective's own husband is under investigation.'

'Yeah.' Chloe laughed.

Jen was confused. Why on earth would Adam pretend to be someone called Sean and spend weeks looking after some coma patient? So, not only did they have to work out how he'd made sales manager, but, more importantly, what his connection to this mystery woman was, too. Why convince her that she was Chloe? None of it made any sense.

'I thought it was the company they were investigating, or at least his business affairs.' Chloe spoke abruptly, as if she'd just thought of it. 'Where does my relationship with him come into it?'

'I honestly don't know. Maybe Hannah just wants to find out how much you know about him.'

'Well, he broke my heart, for starters.'

Suddenly Jen felt desperately sorry for this woman. Not only had she been lied to about her identity, but on top of that, she'd had her heart broken. She kept seeing parallels to what she had done to James.

'Are you okay, Lisa?' Chloe asked.

'Yeah, why?'

'You look totally miserable.'

Jen sighed. 'I was just thinking about James and the kids.'

'Suppose we just split and go out on the town again . . .' Chloe said.

'What? Now?'

'Why not? We could go to Soho or something.'

If only they could! Just get up and walk out of there, like Chloe really was her best friend and not someone who had been given her best friend's memories. Forget all the lying she had done, and the people she had harmed.

'I'd love to, Chlo, but I got in enough trouble the last time I took you out on the town.' God, she wanted to walk away so badly. 'Let's just go back to mine. I'm sure there's something alcoholic in the fridge.'

CHAPTER 83

Chloe Seaward

While Lisa busied herself in the kitchen making alcoholic hot chocolate, Chloe sat on the sofa, her legs drawn up under her, thinking about Sean. She had gone to Lisa in the first place because she wanted to find him, and knew that if he was on record, the service would help. Now that they'd found him, she wondered if she'd made a huge mistake.

'Here.' Lisa came in bearing two mugs. 'One Baileys hot chocolate and cream.'

'Mmm. Just what I needed.' Chloe looked around the room. 'It's nice here, much better than being stuck in that safe house.'

'I couldn't believe my luck when Sam offered to let me stay here. Who knows where I'd be if she hadn't.'

They both sipped at their drinks. After a few minutes, Lisa said, 'We don't have to talk about it if you don't want to.'

'When was the last time someone broke your heart?' Chloe began. 'I mean, *really* broke it.'

'When they told me you'd been killed,' Lisa whispered. 'I kept running through everything in my mind — the way we

203

said goodbye, all the things I should have said to you instead of just walking away.'

'Well, neither of us has ever been good at the big dramatic farewell, have we? It was better for you to just go,' Chloe said.

'I missed you,' Lisa continued. 'I missed you so much it hurt. I'd find myself wondering what you were doing, and if you were safe. Whenever something happened — like when James asked me to marry him — you were the first person I wanted to tell. I'd find myself picking up my phone and then realising you were no longer there to call.'

They fell silent again. 'I thought Sean was going to be my happy ending. I thought I was going to have what you and James had.' Chloe sighed. 'It was all over so quickly. Out of the blue he told me it wasn't working between us, and then he was gone.'

Lisa looked stunned. 'Was he seeing someone else?'

'I honestly don't know. I mean, what makes someone wake up one morning and decide it's all over? After the accident, he told me he'd never leave me, and I was foolish enough to believe him.'

204

CHAPTER 84

Jen Garner

Jen watched Chloe, who was staring into her mug of hot chocolate. She needed to tread carefully. Mindful of what Hannah had told her, she daren't push her too hard, but she needed to know where she had come from, and what for. Adam clearly had some part to play in all this, but what? Why had he left her so suddenly? None of it made sense.

Suddenly, Chloe burst into tears. 'I've never told anyone about him until now. I was determined to hate him, but at the same time I can't forget how he helped me. If it wasn't for him, I might still not know who I really am.'

Jen went over to her, put her arm around her and hugged her tight. 'So, was today the first time since he left that you'd seen him?'

'Yeah, that photo on the tablet.'

'It must have been a shock,' Jen said.

'After he vanished so suddenly, I did wonder if he was on the run from something, or someone. If you're investigating him, I guess he must be.'

Jen didn't know what to say to this.

'What's he done then? It must have been something major to bring him to the attention of the Met.'

Jen sighed. 'You know I can't tell you, Chloe. Ongoing investigation and all that.'

'Bloody service regulations. Anyway, after what he did to me, he deserves whatever is coming to him,' Chloe spat.

'You don't mean that, Chloe.'

'Oh, I do. I can't forgive him.'

'I can understand how you feel,' Jen said. 'Taking advantage of you like that.'

'At least we're together again. Together we're invincible.'

CHAPTER 85

Hannah Littlefair

By now, all Hannah wanted to do was go home and be with her boyfriend, whom she hadn't seen for two days. She had spent two nights crashed on the sofa in her office and was tired and irritable. Chris would probably have gone back to Derby by now. Meanwhile, she had this tangled mess to sort out. Nobody seemed to be who they thought they were — first Chloe and now Adam. How did he fit into it anyway? They were aware that he had been engaged to the dead Chloe, but why had he suddenly surfaced as the false Chloe's husband, and under an entirely different name? They were only keeping an eye on him because they were concerned about his sudden promotion from street drug dealer to sales manager, but with Chloe identifying him, it meant that he was involved in Chloe's reappearance in some way.

Then there was Kristoff, back in the country for who knew what purpose.

Hannah was just about to phone Chris when she received a message from Jen:

Hannah, things have got interesting on the Chloe front. Turns out she was in a relationship with someone called Sean, who we know as Adam Coulthard. As we know, this Chloe was in a coma two years prior to turning up at mine — well, from what she seems to be saying, Sean planted false memories, telling her she was experiencing flashbacks to things from her past in the service. I'm also willing to bet that when this woman came round from her coma, not knowing who or where she was, Sean told her her name was Chloe, and the deception has gone on from there. Then, one day, he told her he was leaving her and walked out, vanishing without a trace. In fact, today was the first time she'd seen him since he left her.

Hannah couldn't make head nor tail of this. Why invest so much time in finding the right girl, brainwash her into believing she was the real Chloe, and then just leave her?

CHAPTER 86

Hannah Littlefair

Hannah was puzzling over the Sean/Adam problem when she received a message from Selina:

> *Boss, I've found information in Chloe's hospital record that I thought you ought to know about. Chloe's real name could be Maria. Her case notes mention that she kept asking about someone called Maria. According to the notes, the husband denied knowing anyone of that name. There's also some interesting reading about Chloe's post-traumatic amnesia episodes, including one where Chloe thinks that someone is checking up on her. Chloe was admitted following a high-speed car crash in November 2021. No other vehicle was involved.*

* * *

'Georgina, Elliot, I need one of you to contact the road traffic department. I'm looking for information on a crash that occurred in November 2021 involving a lone female passenger who sustained severe injuries. I believe she might be our coma patient.'

Georgina nodded. 'I can do that. It'll be a welcome change from looking at trains.'

'Okay, thank you, Georgina,' Hannah said. 'In that case, Elliot, would you access Chessington Hospital's CCTV system for November 2021. You're looking for Adam Coulthard.'

'Which part of the hospital do you want me to focus on?'

'Intensive care, but you might catch him at the main entrance.'

'Okay, Hannah.' Elliot turned back to his computer.

'I'll be in my office if you need me. I'm trying to get hold of the psychologist.'

Hannah rang Dr Spellbound's office, to be told that he was working in London. When Hannah explained that she was calling from there, the woman who answered gave her the number Hannah had just called her on. Wanting to scream, she was finally given a mobile number, which went unanswered.

CHAPTER 87

Jen Garner

'So, what now?' Chloe broke the silence. 'Do we just sit and wait while they hunt down the man I loved?'

'Forget him, Chloe,' Jen said. 'He kicked you to the floor, so why worry about what happens to him?'

How could she tell this woman that the man she loved was really called Adam, never mind the fact that she wasn't really called Chloe, and that everything she knew about herself was a lie? It troubled Jen all the more because what Adam had done to this woman was precisely what she had done to James. How she wished this woman was the real Chloe.

What troubled her most was Adam's motive for deceiving the woman. Was it revenge? If so, what had she done to him?

'Look, I'm tired. I'm going upstairs to have a lie-down,' Chloe said.

'You okay?'

'Oh, I'm all right. It's just that I didn't sleep too well last night, and now with Sean suddenly resurfacing, it's all a bit too much.' Chloe got up and trudged towards the stairs.

Jen was filled with pity for this poor woman. 'Well, I'll be down here if you need anything.'

* * *

Jen got up and went in search of her phone. She knew she wouldn't be able to tell James everything, but at least the sound of his voice might ease her troubled mind. To her surprise, a woman answered.

'Oh, er, hi,' she said. 'Is that James's number?'

'Yes, it is. He's just gone to get a round of drinks in.' What was James doing in a pub with a woman in the early afternoon?

'Shall I get him to ring you back?' the voice asked.

'Yes, do. Tell him it's his wife.'

'Okay then.'

What the hell was going on? The kids were at his parents' place — had he taken advantage of his freedom to hook up with some woman? Upstairs, Chloe was crying. She ought to go and check on her, but she was desperate to hear what James would say.

Finally, her phone rang, 'Sorry, Jen, I was just at the bar. Everything okay?'

'How come you're in the pub? And who was that woman who answered?'

'A friend in need.'

Hmm, enigmatic. 'A friend? What friend?'

'Yeah, Alice. You know her, she's Tom's partner, Tom from work,' he said.

'So, why are you drinking in a pub with her?'

'She's having problems with Tom and needed someone to talk to, okay?'

'It just seems a bit odd, that's all,' she said.

'There's nothing odd about it. I'm sure you'd do the same — except that you're not here.'

'Okay, I'm sorry. I don't want to argue with you.' The last thing Jen wanted was to be a nagging wife.

'When are you coming home?' he asked.
'Soon, I hope. Anyway, better go. Love you.'
'Love you too. I miss you,' he said.
But did he really?

CHAPTER 88

Chloe Seaward

Upstairs, Chloe lay on the bed and was finally overcome by tears. At the sight of that picture of Sean all the hurt he'd caused her had come flooding back. She had never understood the reason for his sudden departure, and now she realised that unless he gave her an explanation, she would never be free of the pain. She needed to confront him, and soon, because if the Met got to him first, she might never get an opportunity. That meant getting away from Lisa. She thought for a moment, then went down to the living room.

'Is it all right if I take a shower?' she asked.

'Sure, help yourself.' Lisa seemed distracted. Good, it would make what she planned to do easier.

'Thank you,' Chloe said. 'I know it's a bit before dinner, but then maybe we can order a takeaway or something? I'm starving.'

Lisa didn't look up from her phone. 'Sounds good to me.'

* * *

Chloe turned on the shower and slunk back downstairs to the kitchen. Grabbing a heavy iron saucepan from the shelf, she tiptoed into the living room, crept round behind Lisa and brought the saucepan down on her head. Her friend crumpled under the blow.

'I'm sorry, Lisa, but there was no other way.' Chloe rolled her on to her side and covered her with a blanket, then went in search of Lisa's bag. Finding her purse, she pulled out several contactless cards — she'd be able to use them to pick up some essentials for her mission. She also moved Lisa's phone, making it harder for her to call for help when she came round.

Luckily, it was still fairly early, so Chloe headed for the nearest supermarket to buy herself a cheap phone.

CHAPTER 89

Hannah Littlefair

At last, Dr Spellbound answered his phone. Hannah explained that there had been some recent developments in the case of Chloe Seaward. 'I could do with your advice, Doctor.'

'Not a problem, Detective. How can I help?'

'We've learned that the woman you assessed for us was in fact a coma patient who was discharged from hospital two years ago. She suffered from amnesia, and we believe someone got to her and planted false memories in her mind.'

'Ah, that might explain the lie detector test,' Dr Spellbound said. 'This person must have known Ms Seaward well, then.'

'He was engaged to the real Chloe Seaward,' Hannah clarified.

'I see.'

'Apparently, the coma patient experienced some post-trau-matic amnesia episodes.'

'Yes, it's a bit like having waking dreams.'

'Well, one of them involved a woman called Maria,' Hannah continued. 'She kept asking who this Maria was.'

'That's likely to be her real name,' the doctor said.

'We think our suspect made her believe that Maria was one of her undercover names.'

'So, how exactly can I be of assistance?' he asked.

'Well, I need to know how to break it to her that she isn't Chloe Seaward. I don't want to cause her any further trauma, though I don't know how it can be avoided,' Hannah said.

The doctor paused. 'Hmm. I see. Of course, it should be done under medical supervision.'

'Yes, I thought that too. Is there any possibility that she'll remember who she was before the accident?'

'Given that she seemingly hasn't had any further memories of her previous life before the accident, I'd say the chances of that happening are exceedingly slim.'

'I understand.' *Poor woman*, Hannah thought. *What kind of life will she have now?*

'I'll speak to some people this end and make arrangements for her to come and stay at one of our facilities. She will need a great deal of help if she is to have a chance of rebuilding her life,' Dr Spellbound said.

'That's good of you, Doctor.'

* * *

'Georgina, Elliot, tell me you've got something positive.'

'It took a while but I spotted him eventually,' Elliot said.

'And? Do we have him leaving with Chloe at any time?'

Elliot shook his head. 'Not so far. In the earlier footage, he looked like he was trying to avoid the cameras, but he seemed to become less bothered about them as time went on.'

'Thank you, Elliot. Georgina?'

'Well, there is CCTV footage of the crash, and it's not pretty.'

'Okay, I don't think we need to see that just now—' Georgina audibly sighed with relief — 'though I wonder why she was driving so fast in the first place,' Hannah said.

'I don't suppose it could have been a suicide attempt, could it?' Elliot asked.

Hannah shrugged. 'Who knows? Given that she remembers nothing from before the accident, that'll probably remain a mystery. What I want to know is what Adam was up to. He can't have spotted her in the hospital, given what Selina says about the security, so where did he find her?'

CHAPTER 90

Jen Garner

Jen came to with a killer headache. How much Baileys had she put in that hot chocolate? Not that much, surely. The pain consolidated itself at the back of her head. Gingerly, she touched the place, which felt wet and sticky. *What the hell?* She took her hand away and found her fingers were covered in blood. Jesus, someone must have got in and attacked her. Suddenly, she thought of Chloe. Had she been attacked too? And what attacker leaves their victim covered with a blanket?

After a minute or two she felt able to struggle to her feet. She called Chloe's name. Nothing. No sound from upstairs. Her head spinning, she staggered over to the switch on the wall. The room was flooded with light. Blinded, she swayed and just made it back to the sofa. Her phone. Where had she left it?

She took a few deep breaths and, still unsteady, looked in all the places she might have put it down. Nope. Her mobile phone was missing, taken by whoever had attacked her? Now she needed to get to Chloe. Taking one step at a time, like a small child, she hauled herself up the stairs. She realised that the shower was still running, but the bathroom was empty. They must have dragged Chloe into her room. No sound came from behind the door. Preparing herself for the worst, she pushed it open. Chloe wasn't there.

She stared at the empty, slightly rumpled bed. No blood. No signs of a struggle. Gripped by panic, she turned, stumbled back down the stairs and checked both the door to the flat and the windows. No indication of a forced entry. Only then did she realise what had happened: Chloe had escaped.

CHAPTER 91

Hannah Littlefair

It had felt so good to pull into her parking space and be home. She looked at the space and wondered if anyone else in the building had noticed that it had been empty for days. She'd heard by text that Chris was still in London, and so she was looking forward to getting into her flat, falling into his arms, having a shower, and then, for the first time in days, falling asleep next to the man she loved.

As she got closer to her flat, she could hear the distant sound of a television and the occasional burst of laughter that could only be coming from Chris. *Home*, she thought to herself. Her safe haven, especially when Chris was there.

'Honey, I'm home!' she called. But there was something different about the flat today. It smelled like Chris's place in Derby after the cleaning company he used had been in. 'What the . . . ?'

'I can explain.' Chris got up from the sofa. Hannah looked around. Her living room was actually tidy!

'Have you been that bored?' Aware that she towered over him with her work heels on, Hannah kicked them off and fell into his arms.

'Well, yeah. I got bored watching TV, so I collected up the rubbish, and one thing led to another—'

'And I have a clean flat.' She pulled away from him and headed for the kitchen area where her days-old coffee cup usually sat.

'Not quite.' Chris laughed. 'I got tired and had to stop, plus your cleaning supplies ran out.'

'Hang on, let me snap some pictures and send them to your cleaners.' Hannah took out her mobile phone and started taking photos, which she then pretended to send on WhatsApp. She didn't say so to Chris, but this was probably the nicest thing that a man had ever done for her, even if she was starting to worry where he'd filed everything away.

'Now all you've got to do is keep it tidy.' Chris brought her close again. 'I missed you.'

'I'd love to say the same, but what with this Chloe case, Tim and bloody Kristoff, I've not had time to think about anything but work.'

'So, is it over? Has Jen gone back to Nottingham?'

'Hardly. I've got two officers undercover — one in a potentially volatile situation. Jen's babysitting a Chloe who isn't Chloe at all, and the rest of us are all completely shattered. I sent everyone home for the night.' Relaxing in Chris's arms, Hannah felt the tension drain away. *Oh, to stay here for ever . . .* 'How are you feeling, anyway? Last time I saw you, you looked completely shattered.'

'I'm good. Apart from a spot of housework, I've been resting, taking my meds like a good boy.'

'Do you reckon they've started to work?'

'I don't know, Han. At least I've not suffered any of the brutal side effects.'

'Good.' She gazed at him lovingly. 'So, what do you wanna do for food?'

He shrugged.

'Well, I need a shower for starters. You can join me if you like, and we'll see where it goes from there.' She eyed him mischievously.

'How about you get in the shower and I'll sort some food?' Chris looked away.

'You know where I am if you change your mind, Detective.' Instead of replying, he started opening and shutting cupboards, taking various items of food from the fridge. She tried unbuttoning her blouse but he wasn't to be tempted. 'Your loss,' she muttered, and headed for the bathroom.

* * *

She hadn't been in the shower long when the bathroom door opened. *Good*, she thought. *He's changed his mind.*

'Hannah, it's Jen.' He held her phone out to her from the doorway.

She took it from him, still dripping. 'Jen, is everything okay? What? Shit. Stay put and I'll be straight over.'

'What's happened?' Chris handed her a towel.

'Chloe knocked her out and disappeared from the flat.'

'Want me to come with you?'

'Erm . . . Yeah, that might be a good idea. Go and start the car while I get dressed. The keys are in my bag.'

CHAPTER 92

Jen Garner

Jen waited for Hannah to arrive, wondering where the hell Chloe had gone. She hadn't checked, but she was pretty sure that Chloe would have taken her cards and any cash she had in her purse.

The screech of tyres below heralded the arrival of Hannah. Jen went to the door and was surprised to see Chris with her.

'So, what happened?' Hannah asked.

'I don't know. I came to with this cut on my head. I had to borrow the neighbour's phone to call you.'

While Hannah hesitated, at a loss for what to do, Chris laid his hand on Jen's shoulder. 'Let's have a look at your head. Hmm. That looks nasty. She must have caught you with the edge of something.'

'Yeah, one of Sam's saucepans. She left it lying on the floor.' Jen grimaced.

'So, how did you let this happen?' Hannah demanded.

'Woah, Han,' Chris said. 'Take it easy.'

'It's fine,' Jen said. She explained what had happened.

'Any idea what time this was?' Hannah asked.

'I'm not sure — about three, I think. Maybe later.'

'That means she's had a three- or four-hour head start on us. Great. I don't suppose you have any idea where she might have gone. No? I thought not.'

'Hannah!' Chris's tone was sharp.

'It's okay,' Jen said. 'It was my fault. I let my guard down.'

Hannah sighed. 'Sorry. I didn't mean to snap at you.'

'All I can think of is that she's gone to find Adam.'

'I hope you didn't tell her where he was.'

'No, I didn't. She kept saying how heartbroken she was after he left her. And I heard her crying after she went upstairs.'

'We should get you to a hospital to get that head injury checked,' Chris advised.

Jen shook her head. 'I'm fine.' Though she had to admit she felt far from fine.

'No, that wound needs cleaning,' Hannah said. 'Chris, would you mind accompanying Jen to Oakmore?'

'Oakmore?'

'It's a private medical facility that the Met uses.'

'Sure,' Chris said. He looked around for her bag and handed it to her. 'Anything missing?'

Jen rummaged around in it. 'She's cleaned me out. Good job my cards were all in Lisa Carter's name.'

'I'll have them traced when I get back to the office,' Hannah said. 'Okay, off you go. Once they've checked that cut and cleaned it up, I guess you'd better come back to base. Chris, you head back home and rest up.'

'Don't we need to be heading to Reading to see if she's gone to Adam's?' Jen asked.

'We can't guarantee that that's where she's going. I'll let Ashley know, and if Chloe turns up, he can take charge of her. Chris, take my car, and I'll get someone from the service to pick me up.'

CHAPTER 93

Hannah Littlefair

As she was driven full speed back to the office, Hannah tried to work out where, yet again, it had all gone so wrong. Maybe she shouldn't have let Jen get involved in the first place. But when you told Jen no, she did the total opposite. She just hoped Chris would be more successful at defusing Jen than she was, but those two had run into a burning building not too long ago, so who knew? She assumed Jen would want to get up to Reading, as Chloe was likely to turn up there, but what if they'd got this whole thing wrong and Chloe had been sent to hurt or maim Jen? She needed to get hold of the teams watching Jen's house and the grandparents, just in case Chloe intended to make a move against the rest of Jen's family. Hannah also needed to call Dr Spellbound again in case she needed his services sooner than she'd previously thought, as well as Ashley's handler, to get the message through that the endgame was upon them. She'd been so looking forward to seeing Chris and lying in his arms again, but Chloe had put a stop to that.

As they pulled into the underground car park, Hannah realised she had the wrong shoes on. Her trainers didn't give her the right air of sophistication, plus they made her short. Maybe she should copy Chris and keep spares in the office, but then she'd end up with as many shoes in the office as she had at home.

Thanking the driver, she got out of the car and headed to the lift. She'd decided not to call the others in. They deserved their rest after working for days on end. She hated being a bitch to Jen, who after all was her friend. Once this was over, they could be close again, but for the time being she needed to keep her at arm's length and act like her boss. If that involved telling her off and pointing out her mistakes, then so be it. Hopefully, Jen was mature enough to understand. Hannah had some powerful people on her back and she couldn't afford to upset them. She'd asked for this job and she had to prove she could handle it, especially when her friends were involved.

As she expected, the office was deserted. Tim, no doubt, had left the second he knew she was out of the building. She turned on all the lights, made herself an espresso, powered up her laptop and got to work. She needed to access the security cameras in the general area of the flat and track bloody Chloe's movements. That is, if she hadn't vanished into thin air. Judging how the surveillance of Kristoff had gone, she was pretty confident of being able to track her. She typed out a quick text to Dr Spellbound, asking him to contact her as soon as possible, and called control, ordering them to check on their teams. She then requested access to Jen's bank accounts to see if any money had been withdrawn, and if so, where. That should give her a good idea of where Chloe was heading.

* * *

Jen Garner

They'd been driving for a while when Jen broke the silence. 'I screwed up, didn't I?'

'Well . . .' Chris hesitated.

'I'll take that as a yes.'

'No, look, I know Hannah's pissed, but that's because she cares. She takes her role very seriously, and blames herself when things go wrong. After all, she could have left you back in Nottingham but she didn't, did she? And in any case, it was her that sent you home with Chloe in the first place.'

'You know they all call her the ice queen in the office?' Jen said.

Chris chuckled. 'I'm not surprised. But you know what? She'll spend the night in that office, alone, because the others need their rest. Instead of giving the job to somebody else, she'll be checking the surveillance systems, following up on Adam. And she'll be making sure your family is watched, so that they're safe from harm.'

'I wonder if I should call James,' Jen said.

Chis shook his head. 'I wouldn't. Given the time, he'll be heading to bed shortly. A call from you telling him you're on your way to hospital would only worry him.'

'I guess you're right.'

Chris leaned forward, peering through the windscreen. 'Now where is this place? It must be around here somewhere.'

'We could always skip this check-up and head to Reading.' Jen couldn't mask the hope in her voice.

Chris grinned. 'That ain't gonna happen. Nice try, though.'

Ahead of them, between the trees, the lights of a building came into view. 'I think that's it,' Chris said. They turned into a driveway and pulled up outside what looked like a large house.

As Chris switched off the engine, a woman appeared in the doorway. They got out and mounted the steps towards her.

'Jennifer Garner?' the woman asked. 'If you'd like to follow me, please.' Chris started forward, but the woman held up her hand. 'I'm afraid you'll have to wait in the car or come back in a couple of hours' time. Out-of-hours regulations.'

About to protest, Chris sighed heavily. 'Okay. I'll wait in the car.'

The woman had already turned away. 'All right, Ms Garner, we'll get your head scanned and that cut cleaned up.'

'Scanned?' Jen asked. 'Is that really necessary?'

'Yes, we need to make sure there're no internal injuries. Follow me, please.'

CHAPTER 94

Chloe Seaward

Having made it out of Central London, Chloe was now sitting in a shop doorway trying to locate Sean using the phone she'd bought earlier with one of Lisa's cards. Thanks to her training she'd been able to avoid the CCTV cameras, until she realised that the best way to remain anonymous was to hide in plain sight among the homeless. She still felt guilty about hitting Lisa, and was worried that she'd struck her too hard. What if she'd done her serious damage? Several times she had been tempted to turn back and check, but it was too late for that. She had to find Sean.

Chloe had googled his name hundreds of times already with no results. But she didn't know where else to try. All she'd seen of him was that picture on the tablet. Had anyone mentioned him at the office? If they had, she couldn't remember it.

Hopelessly, she gazed around at the dreary shopping centre. Caught in the breeze, a newspaper fluttered towards her and wrapped itself around her leg. As she pulled it away, she spotted an advert for a car company headed with the logo she'd seen on Sean's top in the photo. Was the answer to where Sean was about to present itself to her, as if by fate? The advert was for a company called Greenwing Automotive. Eagerly, she looked at her phone and found from their website that they were based in Reading. But did Sean work there? Wearing a T-shirt that had their logo on it didn't necessarily mean that he did, but something was telling her to click on the Management Team, and there he was staring back at her. This was clearly meant to be! But the image bore a different name. Dismissing this as a mistake by the website designers, she headed for the railway station.

CHAPTER 95

Jen Garner

Sporting a bald patch but cleared of any lasting damage apart from a slight concussion, Jen got out of the car at the office. 'Coming?'

'I guess. Though I was under strict instructions to stay safely at home,' Chris said.

Jen grinned. 'Well, she can always kick you out again.'

The building was dark as they entered, the only light coming from Hannah's office.

'I told you she wouldn't call the others in,' Chris whispered. 'It's quite eerie, how empty this place is.'

Hannah was at her desk, eyes glued to her screen.

'Found anything?' Jen asked.

'Oh, hi.' Hannah stood up and stretched. 'What time is it, anyway?'

'Five? Six maybe.'

Hannah rubbed her bleary eyes. 'Everything go okay at Oakmore?'

Jen laughed. 'If anything else happens to me, promise you'll send me back there. But what about you? Found her yet?'

'Yes and no.' Hannah sighed. 'As we suspected, Chloe went straight to a supermarket and spent as much as she could on your cards.'

'Hope she collected my Clubcard points,' Jen joked.

Hannah ignored her remark. 'All in all, she spent £100 on each of your cards.'

'So, do you know where she is now?' Jen said.

'Well . . .'

'You lost her.'

'She was on a train destined for Maidenhead. After that, she disappeared. I can guess where she got off, though, because what isn't far away from Maidenhead?'

'Reading,' chorused Chris and Jen.

'But how does she know that's where Adam is?' Jen asked. 'I promise I didn't tell her. I didn't even let her see that photo again. We just talked about how he broke her heart.'

Chris frowned. 'So, if that's the case, why not get a unit down there to intercept her? What are we waiting for?'

'But if we've already got an officer in the car company, can't he deal with her?' Jen countered.

'And what if she isn't going there?'

Yet again, Hannah was undecided. 'Well, there is a slight possibility that she may have gone to Sean's address — that's where she went when she was discharged from hospital. Chris, you take Georgina and go there.'

'Isn't that a bit of a wild goose chase?'

'We've got to cover all options, Detective. Go on, you know how impressed Georgina was the other day. Take her out for a drive.'

Chris looked at her askance. 'If you say so.'

'Jen, we're going to Reading, but I need to get hold of Dr Spellbound first because he wanted to arrange for Chloe's care after she's told the truth about herself.'

'I guess I should warn my family,' Jen said.

'No, don't worry them. They are being watched,' Hannah reassured her.

Jen got to her feet. 'So, when do we go?'

'Go back to the flat and get yourself cleaned up. I've got some stuff to do here and then I'll meet you in Reading.'

CHAPTER 96

Jen Garner

Seated beside the driver on her way back to Sam's flat, Jen contemplated everything that had happened since Chloe had turned up on her doorstep. How had she got it so wrong? How had she let herself be convinced that this woman was the real Chloe? And not only that, but taking her out to get drunk without informing anyone of what she was doing. She must have been mad.

Needing to hear James's reassuring voice, she pulled out her phone and called him.

She couldn't believe her ears when the same woman answered.

'Hi, Jen. James is just in the shower.'

In the shower? This was worse than she'd thought. 'What are you doing in my house?'

'Oh, James let me stay over last night.' The woman's tone was bizarrely casual. 'Want me to get him for you?'

Jen cut the call, noticing the amused expression of the driver, who would no doubt be relaying the news of her marital difficulties to the entire Met.

It seemed that she'd got this wrong, too. She should never have come back to London. Her phone rang. It was James.

'Hey, sorry, I was in the shower.' He said it as if nothing was wrong.

'What's that woman doing there?' Jen demanded.

'Oh, you mean Alice? Like I said, she fell out with Tom. She has nowhere to stay, so I said she could come here until she found somewhere. After all, there's plenty of space here now I'm all alone.'

'Oh really. Sure you didn't get drunk in the pub and fall into bed with her?'

'Jen!'

'Don't "Jen" me. I'm surprised she wasn't in the shower with you. Anyway, I'd better leave you two to it. Oh, and I may be back tomorrow, so I hope she's found somewhere else to live by then.'

Jen ended the call.

Now what had she done? She was making one mistake after another. James wouldn't cheat on her — she was being totally unfair. She hit redial, but it went straight to voicemail. She tried again, with the same result. Shit! She needed to turn around and go home now to beg his forgiveness.

CHAPTER 97

Chloe Seaward

Having arrived in Reading, Chloe was now standing outside the entrance to Greenwing Automotive. It was early — too early for the managerial staff to have arrived. By now Chloe was practically asleep on her feet, not having slept since leaving the flat. She kept telling herself that all she had to do was have it out with Sean, and then she could return to London with her tail between her legs. No doubt she'd get a tap on the wrist and a suspension, but she was a valuable officer and there weren't many of them around.

* * *

Hannah Littlefair

Meanwhile, Hannah was on her way to Reading, having packed Chris and Georgina off to Chessington.

Her phone rang. 'Detective, I didn't expect to be hearing from you again. It's Tony here from the Reading constabulary.'

'Ah, DI Fox. Good to speak to you again.'

'What can we do for you this time?'

'I need help with Adam Coulthard again, I'm afraid,' Hannah said. 'It seems he's back in your area. I just wanted to let you know that we're on our way over. I didn't want to be trampling over your patch without giving you a heads-up.'

'No problem. I'm always happy to help you guys out.'

'Thank you, DI Fox.' As briefly as she could, Hannah explained the Chloe situation and that she was en route to Reading to attempt to see Adam.

'Wow! That's some case. Risen from the dead, eh?' He chuckled.

'Do you think you could get a team over to where Adam lives? I'm about to get a search warrant.'

'I'll head there myself.'

'Thank you, DI Fox. Maybe you could also listen out for any calls to Greenwing Automotive.'

'Of course. Would you like me to send a patrol car there now?'

'No, I've got an officer there, and I'd rather not spook the poor woman.'

'Not a problem, Detective, I'll get it organised.'

'Thank you, DI Fox. We should be able to contain the situation without bothering your team.'

As Hannah ended the call she noticed several missed calls from Jen. Ignoring these, she instead phoned Dr Spellbound.

'Detective Littlefair, I was about to return your call.'

'Sorry to chase you up. I just wanted to let you know I'm on my way to Reading.'

'Good. I've arranged somewhere for her to stay once you've brought her back.'

'Brilliant. I was wondering how best to handle her. I don't want to have to drag her away by force.'

'Hmmm. I think the best thing would be if I came to Reading and dealt with her myself.'

'Thank you very much, Doctor. We could meet at the entrance to the industrial estate where Adam's company is located.'

'I'll meet you there then, Detective.'

Hannah was about to call Jen when her phone rang.

'Everything okay, Detective?'

'Ma'am, we have a situation here . . .'

CHAPTER 98

Chloe Seaward

The staff of Greenwing Automotive were now trickling in through the entrance. All weariness gone, Chloe stood, tense and expectant. Finally, a black Mercedes pulled up in the car park, and there he was, emerging from the driver's side followed by two women in short skirts.

Chloe ran towards him, calling out his name. But Sean merely glanced at her, frowning. She stopped dead in front of him. 'Sean, it's me.'

'Excuse me, love.' He brushed past her.

Chloe stared at his retreating back for a second or two, then ran after him. 'Sean, why are you doing this to me?'

By now he was mounting the steps up to the entrance. 'Sean, please!'

'You okay, miss?' A security guard had his hand on her arm, holding her back.

'I just want to talk to Sean,' she said.

'I'm afraid there isn't anyone here with that name, love.'

'But there he is!' Chloe shook off his hand and pointed.

'No, love, you're mistaken. He's not called Sean.'

'But he is! Sean! Wait.' But with a single backward glance, he went inside, and the door closed behind him.

Chloe started banging on the door, tears pouring down her face. Someone, presumably one of the other employees, was speaking to her. 'Can I call anyone for you? Here, why don't you come and sit down and I'll get you a glass of water.' Chloe gave up her attempts and allowed herself to be led away.

'I don't understand. Why is Sean pretending he doesn't know me? We were married and lived together for years, until . . .' Chloe broke down.

'But he's not called Sean. I think you've got him mixed up with somebody else.' Chloe looked into the stranger's kind eyes and wondered if she was going mad.

CHAPTER 99

Jen Garner

Once again, Jen was disobeying orders. Her marriage was more important than this, right? James hadn't wanted her to come to London in the first place, and now she was regretting her decision. Why hadn't she just stayed home like a dutiful wife? But no, she'd wanted it all.

And Alice, of all people. She'd seemed so nice when Jen had met her at the company dinners. The M1 would be quiet at this time of the morning. Thank goodness the driver had been accommodating when she told him of her sudden change of plan, merely heading towards the M1 without asking any questions.

Finally, the dreaded call from Hannah. 'Jen, forget the flat. I need you at Greenwing Automotive as soon as you can get here.'

Jen took a deep breath. 'I'm sorry, Hannah, but I need to go home.' Hannah was silent. 'I think James is sleeping with someone else, and I need to get back and save my marriage.' More silence. 'Hannah?'

'I don't understand you, Jen. I thought you were desperate to be part of this case. Now, on a whim, you say, "Oh, sorry, I'm going home to my husband instead." What the hell's the matter with you?'

'I can't lose him, Hannah.'

'I've got no time for your relationship problems.' With that, Hannah ended the call.

CHAPTER 100

Ashley
Greenwing Automotive

At reception, Kim and the two girls were giggling. 'Where'd you get that one from?' Kim nodded towards the door.

'I know, right?' Adam said. 'It's always me they come after.'

One girl was looking out through the glass doors. 'Looks like Benji's sorting her out.'

Adam laughed as he walked away towards his office. 'Good old Benji.'

Ashley had known she was coming. They were on a collision course, but he hadn't expected it so soon. He'd been hoping the team would have got to her first. How was he supposed to deal with the situation now? Walking into the reception area, he went to the water fountain to get the woman a drink and some tissues. She'd been so convinced that Adam was this Sean guy, it broke Ashley's heart because she was right. She was stripped back down to a vulnerable girl. Nothing like the "Chloe" Jen had brought into the office only a few days ago.

'Who is she then, Benji?' Kim asked.

'A case of mistaken identity, I think. She's pretty torn up about it,' he replied.

Kim shook her head. 'She must really have loved this guy.'

'Yeah. I'll take her this cup of water and then come back and see if I can get Adam to talk to her,' Ashley said.

'Might be a good idea. Tell her to come and sit inside with me, and I'll see what I can do. Take her some tissues.' She handed over a box.

'Thank you, Kim. I'll get her now.'

Outside, he offered Chloe the water and the tissues. 'Is there anyone I can call for you? Is there someone who can come and collect you?' She looked up at him, still sobbing. 'I'm Benji, by the way.'

She sniffed. 'Chloe.'

Having told Kim he'd bring her inside, he was reluctant to let her get too close to Adam. 'Chloe, I think you've got the wrong person. That guy is the sales manager, and he's definitely not called Sean.'

'We were married,' she said. 'I can't be mistaken. I don't understand.'

Just then, Kim called to him from the door. 'Benji, love, Adam wants to see you in his office.'

Ashley nodded. 'Let him know I'll be there in a minute.' Telling Chloe to stay where she was, he made his way to the entrance. He had almost made it to the door when he heard a bang and the tinkle of broken glass. Chloe was standing by Adam's Mercedes with a wheel brace in her hand.

'No! Chloe!' Ashley ran back and tried to snatch the heavy object from her hand. She swung it, and he was forced to duck. He saw that Chloe's hand was bleeding — she must have put it through the windscreen as she struck it.

'Kim!' he called out. 'Dial 999 and get the emergency services here.' Turning back to Chloe, Ashley had a sudden brainwave. 'Chloe, Lisa's on her way to help you.'

Chloe lowered the weapon. 'Lisa?'

'Yeah, she's heading here right now.'

Chloe stood, apparently at a loss. Gently, Ashley guided her away from the car and sat her down on a concrete bench. He draped his suit jacket around her shoulders and stood by her side, listening for the wail of sirens.

CHAPTER 101

Hannah Littlefair

Hannah had almost reached the industrial estate when Tony Fox called. 'We've received a report of someone damaging a car over at Greenwing. I'm guessing it must be your woman.'

'Thanks, DI Fox, I'm almost there.' Minutes later, she pulled into the car park where she saw Ashley standing beside Chloe, a short distance from a windscreen-less black Merc.

To her relief, Dr Spellbound arrived at the same moment. He was about to speak when the door to the building flew open and Adam came storming out.

'What the fuck have you done to my car?' he shouted.

As soon as she saw him, Chloe got to her feet. 'Sean!'

'Stupid bitch, I'm not Sean.'

'You said you loved me.' Chloe shouldered her way past Ashley and marched up to him. 'Why are you pretending you don't know me?'

'Because I don't,' he said.

Hannah threw a glance at Dr Spellbound, who began to move toward Chloe.

'Okay, Adam. It's time you explained all this.' Hannah gestured towards Chloe and, beyond her, the smashed-up car.

'I might have known you'd show up,' he said.

'Chloe,' Hannah began. 'Dr Spellbound's here, he's going to take care of you.'

'I'm sorry, Hannah, I just wanted to know why he left me like he did.' Chloe started crying again. Behind her stood Dr Spellbound, a syringe in his hand, ready to sedate her.

Hannah turned back to Adam. 'I'm waiting, Adam.'

'I don't know what you mean. I've not done anything. If anyone needs to explain what's going on, it's her.' He pointed to Chloe.

'Weren't you satisfied with all you'd got from Chloe after she died?' Hannah said to him. 'You had all her life insurance money, and a pretty big pension to boot. I suppose you shot all that up your arm. What was it, revenge? Was that it?'

Adam laughed. 'Oh, but I was good, wasn't I? I had you guys all fooled. I wish I'd seen the look on super cop's face when Chloe turned up on her doorstep.'

Chloe stared at him, uncomprehending.

'But you had bigger things to worry about, didn't you, like how a small-time drug dealer suddenly got to be sales manager,' he said.

Hannah was baffled. 'But why? Why go to all that trouble if it was just to fool us?'

Ignoring her question, Adam continued. 'I bet you were all panicked over super cop's safety.'

'But I loved you,' Chloe wailed.

'Shut up,' Adam growled at her. 'Is that where super cop is now, all tucked up nice and safe? Can't have her chasing after me, can we? She might come to harm.'

'Can't you see what you've done to this woman?' Hannah demanded. 'You've pretty much destroyed her life. Did you not think for a second that she might have a family somewhere, wondering what happened to their girl?'

'She was alone in this world like I was when you took Chloe away from me.'

247

CHAPTER 102

Jen Garner

Having been sat in rush-hour traffic trying to get out of London, Jen started to have second thoughts. The real Chloe had been her best friend, and being with this other Chloe had felt like she'd got her back. Wearily, the driver did as he was told and turned the car around again.

They pulled up in the car park outside Greenwing Automotive. Jen saw a small crowd gathered just outside the entrance, along with police cars and an ambulance. Apologising profusely to her driver, she climbed out of the car and made her way across. In the midst of all the commotion, the small figure of Chloe sat on a bench, crying.

Jen pushed her way through until she was standing in front of her friend. 'Come on, Chloe, you don't need this waste of space.'

'Oh, look who it is! The hero of the hour,' Adam sneered.

Jen turned her back to him. 'Do you really want to be in a relationship with a little prick like this?'

'I just wanted to know why he left me,' Chloe wept.

'Look at him, Chloe, he is nothing but a worthless piece of shit.'

'But I love him.'

'There are plenty of better men out there. Men that deserve someone as beautiful and clever as you.'

'Well, I'll leave you to discuss how worthless I am,' Adam said. 'I've got work to do. Come on, Benji.'

'You're not going anywhere, Adam Coulthard.' One of DI Fox's officers took hold of his arm. 'Other than to the nick, that is.'

'You can't do that. I haven't done anything wrong,' Adam fumed.

'Let's start with impersonation with intent to commit abuse, shall we?' The officer cuffed Adam and led him away.

'Come on, Chloe, it's over.' Jen put her arm around Chloe's shoulders and helped her to her feet. As she stood, Dr Spellbound administered the sedative and, between them, they guided Chloe to the ambulance.

Jen stood at the doors to the ambulance while they made Chloe comfortable inside. 'Aren't you coming too?' Chloe asked. 'Please, Lisa.'

'I just need to sort something out with Hannah and I'll be right with you.' Jen backed away, ashamed at the lie. Chloe gave her a wave, then the doors closed, and she knew she'd never see her friend again.

Jen watched the ambulance disappear, and then turned to face Hannah.

'I see you changed your mind,' Hannah said.

Jen shrugged. 'Even if she wasn't the real Chloe, she still felt like my best friend. And anyway, whether or not my marriage is doomed, I'm still going to need a job.'

Hannah said nothing. Taking her phone from her pocket, Jen stepped away and called James. Even if it was hopeless, she needed to hear the sound of his voice.

'Do you want me to pick the kids up on my way home?' she asked.

'No, Mum's bringing them back tomorrow,' he said.

'Love you.'

He didn't answer for what felt like an age. Then, 'Love you too.'

CHAPTER 103

Hannah Littlefair

'We meet again, Detective Littlefair.' DI Fox held out his hand.

'Ah, DI Fox. Did you manage to carry out the house search?' Leaving Jen to work out what to do with her life, Hannah had followed the car taking Adam to Reading police station.

'We did, and we made some interesting finds. Come to my office — we can talk more easily there.' Hannah followed the DI along the corridors she'd once known so well. It had been many years since she had last been in this station, but it hadn't changed at all.

'Can I get you a drink?' DI Fox asked. 'Coffee? Tea?'

'No, I'm good, thank you.'

'I'm waiting to hear what's on Coulthard's computer, but, along with the expected drug paraphernalia, there were boxes of photos of Chloe Seaward, and a number of notebooks that appear to be some sort of diary,' he said.

'Have you had a chance to look at them yet?'

'The handwriting wasn't Coulthard's — we have a couple of samples of his from when we were looking at him for drugs. These were written by your Chloe Seaward. I had a quick

251

look at the dates, and they run from when Lisa Carter left the service until just prior to Detective Seaward's death.'

'Would I be able to take them back to London with me?' Hannah asked.

'Of course,' he said. 'Now, to Coulthard. When would you like to interview him?'

'As soon as possible. Would you be free to sit in with me?'

He nodded. 'Certainly, if you think it would help.'

CHAPTER 104

Jen Garner

Still thinking of James, Jen checked into the Lothbrook Hotel. She wondered whether it was worth ringing him again and asking him to meet her there. They could have a night away, do all the things they used to do in random hotels in their early days together, just to try and regain that old spark. But that spark had been well and truly extinguished when she chose to go away and chase after her old best friend. Maybe she'd just wait until she finally made it back home and into his arms. The kids weren't due back until the following day, so they'd have plenty of time to talk things over. Her decision was made for her when she called him and he failed to pick up.

She looked in the mirror and wished she hadn't. A tired, haggard woman stared back at her. She needed to sleep, but more important, she needed to see this case to the end. Adam would be at the station by now, being prepared for interview. How would that go, she wondered. How did he know so much about the real Chloe and what she had been up to?

Having been reunited with her credit cards, she'd popped into Primark to pick up something to change into. She ignored the stares of people eyeing her blood-encrusted jeans, and the way they moved aside if she came too near.

She'd jump in the shower, make use of the free hotel samples, grab some food and be back at the Reading station to say goodbye to Hannah before heading home. She couldn't rid her mind of the small figure of the woman she'd believed was her best friend, waving to her from the back of the ambulance while Jen lied to her again, promising to see her soon. Jen wished her the best, whoever she was, and hoped she'd be able to regain her true identity.

* * *

Hannah Littlefair

At Reading police station, Hannah, with DI Fox by her side, faced Adam across the table. He sat slouched in his chair, as if he hadn't a care in the world.

'So, you're telling me you did all this just to see if you could?' she asked. 'You must have had something more than that in your mind.'

He shrugged. 'It worked, didn't it, my *experiment*?'

'Experiment?' Hannah repeated.

'Sure, why not?' Adam turned towards DI Fox. 'Take Detective Littlefair here. She's got a nice arse, and her tits are okay—' Adam's eyes travelled over her body as if she were a new car he was appraising — 'but she's not perfect, is she? What if I said you could create a perfect woman? It's not that hard, actually. All you need is someone who's lost their memory — a coma patient is ideal — and an identity. See, I knew everything about Chloe, she used to tell me everything, and then there were diaries she wasn't meant to keep, and you won't believe how much she revealed in her sleep. So I thought, why not use her to make a replica? Fake documents are so easy to pick up these days, especially when you know the sort of people I do.'

'But you spent years on it,' DI Fox began.

'Once I met this girl in Chessington who was a spitting image of Chloe, it became a sort of obsession.'

'Right.' Hannah and DI Fox exchanged a glance. 'Go on,' the DI said.

'They say everyone has a double somewhere. Well, I found Chloe's, and the rest followed from that.' Adam hesitated. 'Yeah, okay, there was a bit more to it.'

'I thought so,' Hannah said. 'So, tell us. What was your real reason?'

'To get back at you,' Adam snarled. 'You killed Chloe. You left her out in the field alone with no support, until the inevitable happened and someone killed her.'

Hannah bit back her retort. 'So, you took advantage of the situation. Didn't you spare a thought for the woman whose life you've messed up?'

He shrugged. 'She had a better life with me than the one she had before.'

Hannah was in disbelief. 'You couldn't know that.' It was all she could do not to get up from her seat and hit him.

'No one came looking for her, did they?'

'Why would they? You changed this girl's name so anyone looking for Maria wouldn't be able to find her. I can assure you, Adam, that you're going to be in prison for a while, so you'll have plenty of time to wonder if it was all worth it. You've ended up in the very place you told us Chloe saved you from.' Hannah stood up.

'Looks like you'll be staying here for a while, Adam, while we decide what to charge you with,' DI Fox said.

Outside the interview room, Hannah found Jen waiting for her. She had been listening in on the interview through a one-way mirror.

'It's all pretty messed up, isn't it?' Jen said. 'Was he really that obsessed with Chloe that he needed to create a replica?'

Hanah shook her head. 'I don't know, Jen.'

'Let's get some air, shall we?' Jen suggested.

Outside the station, Hannah turned to Jen. 'I'm sorry I haven't been much of a friend lately. I know there've been times when you've needed someone to talk to about James, but I'm here now, okay?'

'Thanks, Hannah, and I'm sorry too. I thought I knew better, but I didn't, did I? Well, I've learned my lesson, and I'm truly sorry for railroading the enquiry.'

Hannah laughed. 'Don't worry. I was warned.' They stood in silence for a while, then Hannah said, 'You know the worst part of it all?'

'What?'

'That we still have no clue who this girl even is.'

'Yeah, I keep wondering about that. The name Maria does keep coming up, though,' Jen said.

'Hopefully, now we know where Adam picked her up from, I can get the team on it. Get her reunited with whoever she left behind.' Hannah paused. 'And, Jen?'

'Yeah?'

'You know you can never see her again, don't you?'

'I know. Anyway, I'll be back home in Nottingham, miles away, trying to rebuild my marriage.'

'Safe travels, Detective. I'll look you up next time I'm in Nottingham, though I'm sure Chris will keep me updated on your escapades.'

Jen gave a weak chuckle. 'If I've still got a job.' They hugged. 'Until next time, Detective.'

CHAPTER 105

Chloe Seaward

Chloe was sitting up in a hospital bed. Her hand, which she'd cut while smashing Sean's windscreen, was still bandaged. But the injury wasn't very serious. Chloe was here for another reason. It was slowly beginning to dawn on her that from the moment she'd regained consciousness following the coma, she'd been living in a dream. From Sean's reaction when she confronted him, she'd worked out that she might not be who she thought she was. But who was she, then?

She was watching the approaching twilight through the large picture window in her room when somebody tapped on the door. She sighed, expecting to see one of the staff come to examine her yet again. But the woman who opened the door wasn't a nurse, or a doctor.

'Lisa?'

Lisa put a finger to her lips. 'Shh. I'm not supposed to be here, but I couldn't leave without saying goodbye.'

'So you're real. There really is a Lisa,' Chloe whispered. 'It's just . . . everything's been so strange.'

'Yes, I am real. And I am your friend. Don't worry, you will get your life back. It'll just take a bit of time,' Lisa said.

Chloe smiled through tears. 'Thank you for looking after me. At least that part was real, wasn't it?'

'It was. And you're safe now.' Lisa walked over to the bed and held her tightly. Both of them were crying now.

Then, with a last smile, Lisa vanished from Chloe's life.

* * *

Once she was clear of the hospital grounds, Jen took the piece of paper with the address of the hospital written on it and ripped it into tiny shreds. She sent a quick text to Hannah saying *Thank you*, and went off to find the long-suffering driver who was to take her home. This time she wouldn't be turning back.

CHAPTER 106

Hannah Littlefair

Hannah opened the door to her flat, wondering what was about to meet her. She remembered the last time Chris had been here. He'd done some sort of tidying, and she'd wondered how the hell she was going to find anything ever again. To her relief he was snoozing on the sofa, still holding a coffee cup balanced precariously on the arm. He looked so peaceful, she hesitated to wake him. Especially as she had just sent him all the way to Chessington on a wasted journey with one of her keenest detectives.

Chris sat up. 'All over then, is it?'

'Sorry, I didn't mean to wake you.'

'Oh, I wasn't asleep,' he lied.

'Oh, right. Well, I'm going to jump in the shower.' Hannah went into the bedroom, relieved to find her dressing gown where she'd left it. She was glad Jen had been able to say goodbye to Chloe. She just hoped she would stay away and give the girl time and space to heal properly.

She still smarted from Adam's accusation that they'd left Chloe out in the field alone and unsupported. She resolved to make it her mission to ensure that this would never happen again.

Shower over, she joined Chris on the sofa.

'Chris, do I talk in my sleep?' she asked.

'Sometimes. Why?'

'Oh, it was just something Adam said today. It made me wonder.'

'Well, he's welcome to come and try to decipher your mumblings, because I sure as hell can't.'

'No state secrets coming from me then.'

'Not a chance. Anyway, I never listen. I'm always distracted when you do that thing where you crinkle up your nose. It's kinda cute.' Hannah gave him a playful cuff.

'Dinner?' Chris asked. 'Though I'm not sure what there is in that fridge of yours.'

'Will you just sit and hold me for a bit?' she said.

'I thought you'd never ask.' Chris put his arms around her. 'Love you.'

Warm in his arms, Hannah closed her eyes and they both drifted off.

She awoke with a start to the sound of her phone.

'Ma'am, I'm sorry to bother you, but we have a situation involving Kristoff. He's at Moreways shopping centre holding a bunch of people hostage, and is demanding to speak to whoever is in charge.'

CHAPTER 107

Jen Garner

Jen hesitated outside her door for a moment, wondering what she would find. Taking a deep breath, she opened it and lugged her bags into the hallway. The house was silent. Too silent. So where was James?

'Honey, I'm home,' she called.

Then she heard his voice from the kitchen. 'I'm in here, love.' Tentatively, she made her way to the door. Was he alone?

James sat hunched over his laptop, his back to the door. She went up behind him and kissed the top of his head.

'Bloody computers. I thought I'd better bring my work home so I'd be here when you got back. Chloe not with you?'

'No, she's in some hospital in the middle of nowhere. We won't be seeing her again.'

'Does that mean it's all over?'

'It is. And, James—'

'Hush.' He stood up and put his arms around her. 'Sorry I missed your call. Work's been hell.'

'Yeah, about that—'

'Shhh.' James held her tightly and kissed her. There was nothing more to be said.

THE END

ACKNOWLEDGEMENTS

Though this book is dedicated to those three amazing ladies I can't let this opportunity go by without thanking them again for making my dreams come true.

I want to thank all the Choc Lit authors who have been as supportive as ever: Ella for reading a genre that she doesn't even like and setting me back in the right direction, Anni for trying to teach me how to write a synopsis that isn't several pages long, Sue for being on hand to help me make bookmarks, Kirsty for all the support with my edits.

Team Joffe: Jasper, Emma, Jasmine and Abbie who have all made the transfer from one publisher to another seamless.

My editors for working their magic and making sure everything sparkles.

Creatives@Coggs that entertain and enlighten me every month with their support and friendship.

Phil Johnson, Angela Leightley, Lucy Mitchell, Cathryn Northfield, Philippa Buchanan, Holy Lord, and as always Jimmy Eat World who after a day of singing my heart out helped me correct everything that was going wrong.

No strange questions with this one, but I'd better thank my amazing MS consultant Dr Nikos Evangelou — no starring role I'm afraid but never far away from Chris' or my life.

The crime-writing community, a lot of you are like rock stars to me, and I only wish I had more courage and confidence when I'm stood there in front of you to be like 'Hi.'

The teams behind The UK Crime Fiction Book club and The Fiction Café who have been more than willing to shout out about my books, host me on podcasts, live streams and shout loudly about any book-related news.

Georgina Gascoigne and Tyler Shepherd who helped raised an amazing amount of money for Comic Relief through Child In Read.

Angela Turner, who won a competition to give a gift to Chris, gifting him his adopted donkey.

To my sister-in-law, who took an early copy of this book on holiday to read.

Christine Curtis for casting her eyes over my spelling and grammar and providing regular updates on how much she loved the new book.

My work colleagues who after my family spend the most time hearing about author dramas. Thank you for your positivity, the 'You can't just give up, Claire!' and that time I told you about my next book being about my lost keys!

Lee Anderson: you have to read this one now your name's in it! Don't worry, I'll send bookmarks to remind you.

Grandad: I'm gutted you're not here to read this one, after promising you there was one coming for so long.

To my family: Alex, who will either try and sell you a book or be on hand with a bookmark. Melanie, whose enthusiasm for everything I wish I could bottle and sell and of course Andrew, who once again made no effort in making this book happen, but he loves me so that's all that matters.

NOTE TO READERS

Hey,

This book was submitted just prior to Joffe purchasing Choc Lit so the road to publication has been a bit longer this time, but here we are book 4, *A Dead Lie*.

I never imagined when I was writing this book a close family member and a friend would be put in medically induced comas. Now both fighting fit, their recovery was very different to the one portrayed in this book.

My inspiration for this book came from the thought that there is so much that Jen went through prior to *A Perfect Lie* that we've only scratched the surface of. What if the one person she shared so much with is alive and standing on her doorstep? What would you do if your dead best friend was really alive and stood in front of you? Would you welcome them with open arms, or would you react the way Jen does?

Though we don't see much of Chris in this book, who pretty much sleeps through this book, I don't know one person who has MS that doesn't suffer with the killer fatigue. Plus, early in anyone's diagnosis journey there's the side effects of the drugs while they get the right ones and doses. So, I've given him a well-earned rest but don't worry, he'll be back in the future. Probably just as tired but fighting crime the way he does best.

For more information on MS and where you can find support please go to www.MStrust.org.uk and www.mssociety.org.uk or join the Facebook group muMSUK.

I really hope you enjoyed reading the next book in the Jen Garner series and those who've recently discovered the series please feel free to reach out to me at any time. I love reading all the messages and tweets I get from readers, it really does add sparkle to my day. Gold stars if you spot the Taylor Swift references.

Claire
x

THE CHOC LIT STORY

Established in 2009, Choc Lit is an independent, award-winning publisher dedicated to creating a delicious selection of quality women's fiction.

We have won 18 awards, including Publisher of the Year and the Romantic Novel of the Year, and have been shortlisted for countless others. In 2023, we were shortlisted for Publisher of the Year by the Romantic Novelists' Association.

All our novels are selected by genuine readers. We are proud to publish talented first-time authors, as well as established writers whose books we love introducing to a new generation of readers.

In 2023, we became a Joffe Books company. Best known for publishing a wide range of commercial fiction, Joffe Books has its roots in women's fiction. Today it is one of the largest independent publishers in the UK.

We love to hear from you, so please email us about absolutely anything bookish at choc-lit@joffebooks.com

If you want to hear about all our bargain new releases, join our mailing list: www.choc-lit.com/contact